DON'T BANK ON IT, SWEETHEART

MICHAEL N. WILTON

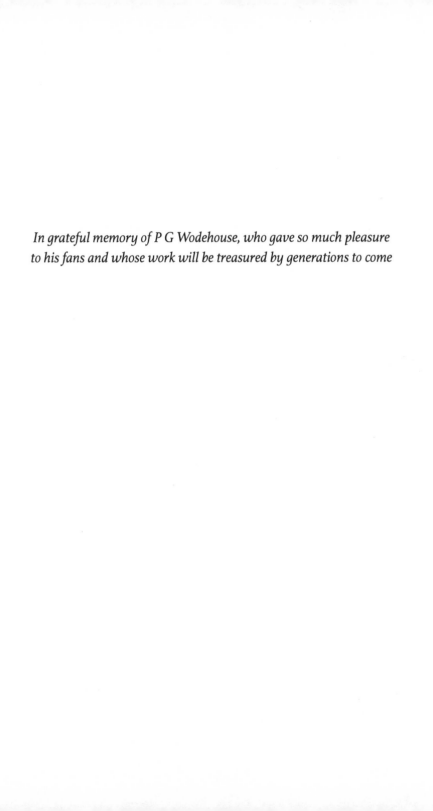

In grateful memory of P G Wodehouse, who gave so much pleasure to his fans and whose work will be treasured by generations to come

A JOURNEY BACK IN TIME

For those of you who don't understand (or don't want to know) what DVD means – or can't stand the sight of someone ringing his loved one on a mobile in the middle of a crowded carriage just to say the train is on time – take heart. Put away those blood pressure pills and come with me on a journey back to a time when life was simple and spartan – before the age of computers and email, where you had to use your imagination to amuse yourself instead of switching on the box.

At last, the war was over, and the world would be a better place for everyone, or so they thought. It was, in that time, a question of what to do to get the country back on its feet again, and how to get started. But with so much competition for jobs, the outlook was bleak for young men of only average intelligence – even less for those like Alastair, George, and Arthur.

Alastair made up for it by sheer egotistical cunning and

affecting a lordly appearance that got him out of scrapes on more occasions than anyone would care to remember. Today, he would have won or lost a fortune as a rogue trader or made a name for himself in politics. He had all the right qualifications – a broad, flexible outlook that reminded one irresistibly of that giant amongst men, Stanley Featherstonehaugh Ukridge, immortalised by P.G. Wodehouse.

George, on the other hand, had no brains to speak of, just an insatiable appetite, and was completely happy as long as he was left alone to pursue his hobby of stuffing his face. The only time anyone saw him really upset was when a dog sneaked a treble-decker sandwich it had taken him all morning to prepare. He got over it by applying for a job next day as a butcher's assistant.

Like so many others at that time, Arthur had no university education. It was wartime, and after his parents were killed in the blitz, he was brought up by a reluctant aunt. Any writing ambitions he may have had cut no ice with Aunt Ciss, who regarded it as a complete waste of time and viewed him as a liability.

After sending out a fistful of hopeful articles and getting snowed under by rejects, Arthur emerged from his tiny garret every evening, after making do with a leftover sandwich and a glass of milk, to be greeted by a continuous tirade of complaints from his Aunt Ciss, which did not help to restore his morale.

As she put it, sitting back comfortably in her armchair and tucking into an enormous plateful of chicken pie between gulps of whisky, "Fat lot of good all that scribbling does for you, young man. What you want is a proper job – something that brings in some real money, not all those silly rejects you keep getting. How do you think I can afford to keep you on top of all those bills that keep on coming in? You've no idea how much everything costs your poor old aunt these days."

"But I was hoping that money Dad left me might be enough to keep me going until I've built up some freelance work..."

She nearly choked over the thought. "You thought it was enough to keep you going? On what, I might ask? That was only enough to pay for a few measly mouthfuls," she said, omitting to mention that it paid for a daily queue of delivery vans that attempted to keep up with her insatiable appetite.

"I do my best, but there aren't enough jobs to be had."

"Nonsense, you're not trying hard enough." Her mind diverted. "What about that nice young girl I introduced you to, Mavis, wasn't it?"

"Mavis?" He shuddered. "She was so fat she couldn't get the rings off her fingers."

"What's that got to do with it? If you married her, you wouldn't have to worry; her father's a merchant banker with oodles of money. I don't know; there's no pleasing you these days. And there was that other girl, Frenela something or other," she added. "She would have made a splendid wife for you. She is a teacher and would have passed on all the social graces you need – of course, her father is well off in the civil service. Not that that has anything to do with it, but if you get in there, you have a job for life."

"I couldn't think of anything worse," argued Arthur. "She was ugly as sin and always giving me good books to read."

"Well, I don't know; you're very difficult to please. I don't know what we're going to do with you."

"Yes, Auntie," he said, getting up wearily. "I'll just have to see what tomorrow brings."

"You do that, Arthur," she said, bolting down another mouthful, "otherwise we'll starve – and you wouldn't like your poor old auntie to be left in that position, I'm sure. If things go on like this," she warned ominously, "I shall have to take in another lodger and we've only got your spare bedroom available, so for goodness sake do something. I don't think you've heard a word of what I've been saying."

"No, Auntie, I mean, yes, Auntie," he sighed.

But it was no better the next day or the day after. Everywhere he went, there seemed to be queues of ex-servicemen looking for work. Reviewing his prospects, he came to the conclusion that as far as his future was concerned, it was either the army or the bank.

In the Blackheath suburbs where he lived, the city was only a short distance away, so it made more sense to try for the bank. The musty confines of that august building at Fleetgate, only a short tube ride from London Bridge, with all its antiquated habits and characters, would give him all the material he needed as a writer to last him a lifetime.

But the prospect of coming home to find Aunt Ciss holding court in the front sitting room every night, waiting to snap at him in bleary hostility at the slightest excuse, filled him with panic. He had to escape. His first step was to get away, anywhere, and find cheap lodgings where he could scribble down some ideas for an article that would hopefully help to pay off some of his mounting bills.

With the rejection slips piling up thick and fast, and rent day looming ever closer, he was saved from bankruptcy by a lucky encounter with an old friend of the family, Alastair Stringer, who he (and most of the family) had always avoided in the past because of his pompous and 'know-it-all' manner.

But he was in no position to be choosy, so on an impulse, he sought Alastair out and asked him humbly if he could help in any way. Adopting an airy manner, his friend waved away any anxieties Arthur might have.

"Lord, yes, I can get you in, old lad. No trouble at all. The manager would do anything for me. Trouble is whether you really want to work in a bank. It's not the sort of career I was expecting myself, you understand. The family wanted me to go in for the Foreign Office, you know. Uncle Henry begged me to take on Gibraltar during the war, but those blasted apes put me off. Always chattering about the place – couldn't stand it. Anyway, if you're sure, I'll look after you. Just leave it to me."

But when it came to it, Arthur found work in the bank deadly boring and longed to become a writer. As he entered the building every morning, the drab surroundings did nothing to dispel the general feeling of gloom that surrounded him. The august bust of Joshua Bullett, the family bank's revered founder, stared coldly down at him from his prominent niche above the counter as if registering his disapproval at Arthur's presence on the staff, and he would slink past with an averted gaze.

The one person in the bank who seemed to know how he felt and listened to him with understanding was – you've guessed it – Alastair. Such a friendly person, Arthur thought. Nothing like the show-off they had always imagined. He was like an elder brother in those first few weeks. Told him all sorts of interesting things about the goings-on in the bank.

"D'you see that messenger of ours, Conrad, old man? You wouldn't think he owned a string of paper stands around the city, would you? They say he pays Head Office his salary because it's handy for him to use this as his base. That would make a better story than all those sea sagas your grandfather went in for."

Arthur's heart warmed towards him. "Well, actually my name is Conway," he reminded. "Arthur Conway – not Conrad. Although," he added shyly, "I do want to write."

"Course you do, old man. It's only a matter of time. Your name will be up in lights, you just wait and see."

By then, Arthur was almost purring with devotion.

"I blame it all on the war," Alastair sighed, shooting a sly look at Arthur to make sure he had his sympathy. "Killed off all the best ones, and look what we've got left. Morrissey, our beloved manager, who's given up any hope of promotion and pretends he's a station master playing at trains. Old Jenkins, our blasted chief clerk, who doesn't think you're fit for anything until you've slaved at the ledger for over fifty years. And Symmonds, our first cashier, who spends all his time dreaming about retirement. As for that slacker Harris, his number two, beats me why he bothers to come in. They've been trying to get rid of him for years. He just nods off over his till every day, and we have to wake him up and remind him when it's time to go home." He shook his head. "The trouble with this world is all the wrong people are in charge. It's them or us. You mark my words, Arthur. One of these days there'll come a reckoning, oh yes. An' then they'd better watch out."

"But what can anyone do about it?" Arthur asked earnestly. For he was without doubt very earnest and naive in those days.

"What can we do about it, you mean? Listen, I'll tell you something I wouldn't tell anyone else." He lowered his voice, and it took on a quavery note. "I don't usually take a shine to people, but I like you, Arthur, I'm not ashamed to admit." He wiped his eyes and peered mistily. "Something I haven't done since my old mother died."

Like an idiot, Arthur grabbed his arm impulsively. "If there's any way I can help..."

"Good man – I knew I could rely on you." Alastair laid his finger on the side of his nose and winked confidentially. "This is strictly between you and me mind, but the job of holding the key to the strong room is coming up for review this week. As you know, two men have to open the strong room together to make sure there's no hanky panky going on. Jenkins, who holds one set of keys, is away with flu and old Symmonds is retiring soon, so they're looking for someone to take it on before then, someone they can rely on in case he drops down dead in the meantime. If I put a word in for you, don't let on, will you? Might be something in it for you. But mum's the word, eh?"

Arthur stared at him, puzzled. "But what's that got to do with the wrong people being in charge?"

His friend seemed to wince at the phrase 'in charge,' then recovered and gave a beam

of encouragement. "All in good time. Now, what d'you say? Come on, it's your big chance."

"Why should they pick me? I've only been here a few months."

"Because they trust you, my boy, that's why. And don't we all?"

He dismissed the worried look on Arthur's face with an airy wave of the hand. "Anyway, with Jenkins off sick, they're short-staffed and it'll save them getting in a temporary replacement. I know that lot – mean as the proverbial monkeys."

"Stringer!" bawled a peevish voice at the back of the office. "Where is everyone, today?"

"It's old Morrissey," hissed Alastair. "Coming, sir!" he cooed in a disgustingly servile manner, then scurried off down the corridor. His honeyed words floated back, "Sir, may I have a few words?" Following on his heels, Arthur was just in time to see the manager snatch off his station master's hat and hurriedly hide a red flag in his desk drawer out of sight.

"Ah, Stringer, everything on track?'

"Sorry to bother you, sir, seeing as you're so busy," he heard Alastair apologise profusely in his usual smooth manner. "You remember you were asking about a replacement for a key holder the other day... I think I might have the answer." Then the door closed in his face, and their voices faded away.

The next few days, Arthur was uncomfortably aware of the manager giving him a searching look as he passed his office before throwing up his hands and putting up a 'Do Not Disturb' notice on the door. He didn't cotton on to this at first, but after catching the manager rushing into the Gents one morning in his stationmaster's hat, he realised his superior was in the middle of retreating into a private world where the Flying Scotsman and the Great Eastern reigned supreme. The second or third time they passed each other, the manager merely shook his head in disbelief. When Arthur mentioned this to Alastair, he looked thoughtful, and soon after, Arthur saw him heading for the manager's office after snatching up a sheaf of papers.

Anxious to learn more, he hesitated by the door as he paused to fetch the tea tray and heard the manager complain, "But he's far too young, why can't you do it – you're his senior."

"Ah, I would if I could, but you know how it is with the old ticker, sir. That reminds me, if you could just approve my medical expenses for last month..."

"Here, where do I sign? Don't you collapse on us," said the manager in alarm. "We're far too short-staffed as it is. Dammit, if only Jenkins hadn't gone down with flu..." Arthur heard him kick at the wastepaper basket in frustration. "How can I appoint someone his age? It took me years to reach that position..."

"Ah, but think how well it will be viewed from above," murmured Alastair.

"How well?" repeated Morrissey hopefully.

"Just think of it, sir. How many juniors have been promoted to the position of key holder at only seventeen?"

"None, as far as I know..." said the manager fearfully.

"I can see it now," prompted Alastair. "That intrepid band of directors meeting in the boardroom, shaking their heads in admiration. Such courage, they are saying. Who is this man, Morrissey?"

"A courageous idiot, you mean," muttered the manager. "More likely they'd fire me."

"You underestimate your abilities, sir," Alastair said

earnestly. "Such a breath-taking step will make them look upon you in a new light. Hm, I can hear the chairman declare, 'We must find room for people like this, not afraid to take bold decisions. When is old what's-his-name retiring as general manager of branches?'"

"General manager?" whispered Morrissey.

"Every age has its born leaders," said Alastair dreamily. "William Pitt, the Younger, was only twenty-four when he became prime minister…"

"He was?"

"It's not too late to make your mark in Head Office. General Manager today, and who knows what fate has in store tomorrow?"

"Dammit, I will." As he came out of a trance, the manager unbent. "You can get up off your knees, Stringer. Send young Conway to me at once. If all goes well, I won't forget your suggestion."

A dazed and triumphant Alastair emerged from the inner sanctum and uncrossed his fingers. "It worked," he crowed unbelievingly.

Catching sight of Arthur, he beckoned excitedly. "Quick, get in there before he changes his mind."

The person most surprised by Arthur's sudden elevation the following Monday was Stuart, the messenger, who dropped his cigar and nearly burnt his finger in astonishment at the idea. As for Symmonds, he had a seizure on the spot when he saw who would be helping him to open the strong room. Arthur felt so nervous at the sudden promotion he could sense the manager's eyes boring through the back of his neck, anxiously willing him to go through the correct procedures of unlocking and locking the massive locks. Even Alastair was hovering in the background, ready to rush forward with advice.

But luck or good fortune was on Arthur's side. He didn't know whether it was the relentless coaching from Alastair or the fear of making a mistake in front of the manager, but he managed to do all the right things at the right time.

Whether word had filtered up to Head Office or not, nobody could hazard a guess, but two days later a white-faced manager dashed out of his office and croaked, "Stringer, where the blazes are you?"

He grabbed Alastair by the arm and hustled him into his office, and Arthur followed discreetly, just out of sight.

"They want me to go to Head Office right away," he blurted out. "What shall I say?"

For a moment, Alastair was taken aback, but he did a quick calculation and said without thinking, "I told them next week, the idiots..." Then he rallied. "There's no need to worry, sir. It just means a change of plan, that's all."

"Change of plan? You mean, I don't get any promotion?"

"No, of course not," said Alastair soothingly. "Everything's going to be fine. This is your big chance, remember? Off you go to your appointment – just keep on repeating 'General Manager' to yourself and everything will be fine."

Morrissey clutched at Alastair's lapels for reassurance. "You're sure about that?"

"Ug, absolutely," croaked his victim, freeing himself. "Remember – 'General Manager.' Oh, and, sir," he added casually, "it might be a good idea if you could leave the other spare set of safe keys with me, in case of emergencies."

"Yes, good thinking," replied Morrissey, glassy-eyed. He sat down heavily and mumbled to himself, "General Manager, General Manager..."

Watching the departing car, Alastair checked his watch with unusual nervousness.

"Right, it's Plan B," he snapped suddenly. "Get your strong room keys, Conrad. Time for action."

"Here, wait a minute..." Arthur objected, slightly confused.

"We've already got the notes and coins out. They don't go back until we close."

"We're not putting anything back, Conrad." He looked around in case he was overheard. "Don't you understand, you idiot?" he hissed. "We're taking it out!"

2

ANSWERING THE CALL

"But-but..." Arthur stuttered, thrown off-guard. "What for?"

Alastair brushed the question aside impatiently. "Can't stop to explain now; we've no time to waste. Any moment now he might find out he's got the dates mixed up and come back..."

Before Arthur could say anything with his mind in such a whirl, his friend hustled him down the stairs and produced the manager's keys and, carefully selecting one, turned it in the keyhole.

"Now yours," he directed. Seeing Arthur's mouth slacken open, he looked at his watch again impatiently. "Come on, we haven't got all day." Then he relented. "Don't you see, Conrad, old man. This is our chance to get back at them."

"What do you mean – 'them'?" Arthur repeated stupidly, beginning to get suspicious despite his loyalty. "Why are we getting any more out – who wants it anyway?"

Alastair began to laugh wildly. "Who wants it, he asks? Why I do...er, we all do, fathead." Then he sobered up, and his eyes took on a cunning gleam. "Why do you want to know?"

"Well, if we haven't got a good enough reason, why... it sounds like stealing." Arthur felt uneasy.

Alastair puffed out his chest. "You're not accusing me of stealing, old man, are you?" he asked in shocked tones, glancing surreptitiously at his watch.

"No, but you haven't told me yet who it's for."

"Head Office, of course. Who else?"

"But why do they want it? We've got to have enough for the customers." Arthur found himself getting persistent. "Surely they realise? They must have a better reason than that."

"Oh, there is, old lad," his friend said soothingly. As he spoke, his eyes took on a hunted look and rested briefly on the box of first aid on a nearby shelf, kept for emergencies. His face lit up at a sudden thought. "Of course, I didn't explain, did I? You must think I'm thick." He laughed indulgently. "It's for the Red Cross."

"Red Cross?" Arthur repeated in astonishment. "What do they want it for?"

Alastair's brow cleared and he launched into a glib explanation. "You've heard about the refugee crisis over there..." He gestured vaguely in the air and hurried on before his statement could be questioned. "You see, it's like this, old man. When the Jerries retreated, they took all the money they could lay their hands on wherever they went. It left thousands without anything. Whole countries were involved; you've no idea. People were left destitute. Starving, old man – absolutely without a bean. In confidence," he lowered his voice, "and don't let this get around, but the Government were left with a revolt on their hands." He staved off the next question that sprang to mind. "Couldn't have that, could they? Stands to reason. We've got to do something before it's too late."

"But what's that to do with getting money out of our strong room?"

Alastair pulled him closer and whispered in his ear, "Special emergency shipment, old man. Got to get it to Croydon Airport, pronto. Every minute counts to stave off the riots. Head Office said so. Can't argue with that, can we?" Swinging the door open, he urged, "Hurry up with that bundle of notes, will you." He wiped his forehead. "If we don't get this done on time, bang goes our promotion, old man."

Arthur listened to his tale with growing misgivings. It all sounded so fantastic, yet there was a possible slim thread of reason behind it all that he couldn't ignore, and his friend could just be right. The papers had been full of it recently, warning of all kinds of disasters to come if the country didn't pull its socks up.

The sheer volume of words that poured out of Alastair after that almost overpowered Arthur, and he found himself following the instructions given to him in a semi-trance like state, piling trays of notes onto the trolley until Alastair glanced triumphantly at his watch and flung his arm up.

"That's it, that's all we have time for. Now, quick's the word. Hurry up," he wheezed, almost choking in his excitement.

With a supreme effort, they pushed and pulled at the trolley until they got it out onto the ramp leading down into the street. Overcome by the exertion, Alastair mopped his brow, and they both leant against the door wearily, shutting it behind them.

While they were still getting their breath back, the trolley gradually began moving away from them in a kind of ponderous slow-motion and started to gather speed. Arthur stood there exhausted, unable to shout or do anything.

"Watch out!" screamed Alastair, catching sight of it. "It's getting away. Stop it!"

At that moment, a butcher's boy doing deliveries appeared around the corner and slowly pedalled towards them in a care-free fashion, totally oblivious of the runaway trolley bearing down on him.

"Roll out the barrel," he carolled, "let's have a barrel of ..."

His eyes suddenly widened. What he was expecting to have a barrel of was never ascertained. At that moment a van decided to back into the yard, and the bicycle wobbled frantically.

What happened next took them completely by surprise. There was an almighty crash as the van rammed into the trolley and caught the bicycle a glancing blow, sending a cascade of meat and vegetables flying up in the air in all directions.

Jumping out of the van, the driver cast a desperate look around. A blast of a police whistle sounded in the next square, and that settled it. In a flash, he bolted down a side street, and two police cars with sirens blaring screamed to a halt from around the corner, nearly ramming the van.

Arthur turned instinctively to his friend to see what he would do now and couldn't help feeling sorry for him. With ruin staring him in the face, he gamely tried to brazen it out.

Staggering down the ramp, he pointed wildly after the van driver and shouted hoarsely,

"Catch that man – he tried to rob the bank!"

In the confusion that followed, the police were trying to stop passers-by from making a grab at the wads of notes fluttering in the breeze, while a group of tourists, attracted by the noise, entered the yard waving their arms and started gathering up the bundles. More motorcycle police arrived and started moving the crowd back as a plainclothes policeman accompanied by a uniformed sergeant moved forward purposefully. At this point, Alastair seemed to give up and started helping the butcher's boy to his feet.

"Detective Sergeant Bird," said the policeman, introducing himself. "Can you explain what is going on here?" He picked up a wad of notes and ruffled through them. "Do you know anything about this?"

Alastair nodded dumbly, then found his voice. Not looking at his friend, he announced in heroic tones that would have wrung tears from any front row matinee. "It was all my doing. I take full responsibility." Then he spoilt it by repeating it all again like a gramophone with the needle stuck.

Unable to bear any more, Arthur interrupted hastily. "Listen, I was helping him as well..."

"Don't take any notice of Conrad. He's too young to know what he's saying." Alastair smiled manfully and squared his shoulders as if ready to take his place on the tumbrel.

The Detective Sergeant looked keenly at both of them in turn and got out his notebook.

"One thing at a time, if you don't mind. Your name, sir?"

Alastair said nobly, "Alastair Stringer..." Then he looked over the policeman's shoulder. "With an 'er', if you don't mind, officer."

Swallowing, Arthur stepped forward to accept his share of the blame. "And I'm Arthur Conway. We both work at the bank."

Snapping his notebook shut, the Detective Sergeant said briskly, "Right then. Would you two gentlemen mind accompanying me down to the station to answer a few questions?"

As they were about to leave, the policeman turned to the butcher's boy as an afterthought. "You didn't happen to see anything, did you, sonny?" The young, red-faced cyclist tried to say something, but there appeared to be an obstruction in his throat, and his eyes nearly bolted out of his head in an effort to get rid of it.

"Gug-gug." Suddenly, a small object, closely resembling a piece of sausage, shot out of his mouth and hit the policeman plumb in the eye.

Breathing hard, the Detective Sergeant wiped his eye. "If you're not careful, my lad, you'll be had up for causing an obstruction."

"No, it was the sausage, Sarg, honest. I deliver meat, that's my trade – look, it says so on my bike, what's left of it."

"Bring them all down," ordered Detective Sergeant Bird grimly.

Arthur's heart sank as the sergeant stepped forward and motioned two policemen to escort them to the car.

Just then, another car screeched to a halt and Morrissey jumped out in an agitated state.

"What's happened here? Thank heavens you got here in time, Inspector. Have you caught the men responsible for all this?" He flung an arm out in outraged indignation at the upturned trolley and scattered money.

"There appears to have been an attempted robbery, sir. These gentlemen are helping us with our enquiries." The Detective Sergeant was non-committal.

Morrissey's face was a picture. He saw the mute appeal in the faces before him and looked at the Detective Sergeant as if he had just caught him out asking for a double-decker loan without any supporting collateral.

"I get a message calling me to Head Office and when I get back – what do I find?" he spluttered. "Money all over the place and the police taking away two of my most trusted senior staff!"

Arthur looked around, wondering who he was talking about, and with amazement, realised the manager meant the two of them. The officer tactfully let go of their arms and stood back.

"It's just routine," he said soothingly. "We have to get a statement from all the eye-witnesses, sir."

"You haven't asked me," piped up the butcher's boy unexpectedly. "I saw it all happen."

"There you are!" The manager straightened up with authority. "Why didn't you ask this young man instead of behaving in this high-handed manner?"

Detective Sergeant Bird took out his notebook again with resignation. "All right, sonny. What did you see?"

The butcher's boy needed no invitation. "There was this

van, see! He reversed back and ploughed right into the trolley with all the money on it, see? Then he hit my bike and sent me for six, see? And then these blokes rushed out and tried to stop him, and the driver did a bunk, see?"

"I see. I mean, what happened then?" asked the officer, licking his pencil.

"All you coppers turned up, didn't you – after he got away."

"Take his name and address, constable," said the Detective Sergeant hurriedly. "Now then, sir, can you tell me what the money was doing out of the bank on this particular day?"

"I expect my staff had a request to transfer some money, isn't that right, Stringer?" said the manager righteously.

Alastair came out of his trance, hardly believing his good luck. "That's right, sir. Head Office rang up five minutes after you left. It wasn't the usual man, Timmins, though," he said, doing some quick thinking. "I didn't catch his name, but he sounded as if he had a cold. Funny that."

"There you are!" Morrissey barked. "It was all a ruse to hoodwink my people and rob the bank. Now, if you'll excuse me, Officer, we are extremely short-staffed, and we have to get that money back in the vault before any other villains turn up."

"Certainly, sir." Detective Sergeant Bird snapped his notebook shut with a sigh. "I'll arrange for some of my men to give you a hand. Perhaps you would be kind enough to come down to the station when you have time to sign a statement."

"Later, officer, later. Now, if you don't mind…"

"Here, wait a minute," piped up the butcher's boy. "Who's going to pay for my bike what got broke?"

"I expect there'll be a suitable reward," said the officer, dabbing his eye. "Better ask these gentlemen."

A look of bliss spread over the cyclist's face. "D'you mean free steaks?"

"I wouldn't be surprised," said Alastair with relief.

"You're on." Thus marked the beginning of a beautiful friendship between George, the butcher's boy, and Alastair.

"It was all a fiendish plot. They must have been waiting for just the right moment to strike while I was out of the office," babbled Morrissey, seizing Alastair by the hand and pumping it. "Thank goodness you were there to stop them."

Looking suitably modest, Alastair murmured, "It was nothing." He kicked his friend in the ankle. "I couldn't have done it without Conrad here."

Arthur stuttered a few words, torn between telling some semblance of the truth to salve his conscience while remaining loyal to his friend. In the end, he gave it up and left it to Alastair who seemed quite content to explain it all away.

"Well, that's all accounted for – all £20,000," said the manager two hours later with great satisfaction, leaning back in his chair. "Now I can tell you my own good news... Stringer, you're not listening."

Alastair reluctantly tore his gaze away from the pile of money. "Sorry, sir," he mumbled. "You were saying?"

Morrissey straightened his tie and tried to tuck his stomach in. "You are looking at the new Assistant General Manager."

"No! The call wasn't a fake then?" He stopped, confused, then battled on. "I mean... you really did get a new appointment?"

"I did, indeed. It was all confirmed only half an hour ago." He blinked. "D'you know, I can hardly believe it."

"Well," said Alastair weakly. "I'm sure you deserve it."

"And what is more, I owe it all to you," Morrissey said, prodding Alastair in the chest,

"and, of course, young Conway here."

Arthur stammered a reply, embarrassed by his part in the fiasco.

"Not forgetting that young butcher's boy, what's-his-name, George, who seems so fond of his food. You can tell him from me I'm treating you all to a farewell dinner tomorrow night at Whites Hotel – and there will be plenty of steaks on the menu – and a bottle of wine to celebrate. No expense spared, I can promise you." He smacked his lips in anticipation.

"Yes, indeed." He looked around cautiously. "And this is all confidential. Just between you and me, mind – I have put both of you in for a rise. No, don't thank me," he said majestically as Alastair jumped up hopefully, his face lighting up. "Let me see, I wouldn't be surprised if you get at least another ten," he did a few quick calculations, "ten shillings a month."

Alastair sank back, too overcome for words, and Morrissey patted him on the shoulder.

"Oh, and I didn't tell you, did I?" He laughed heartily at the recollection. "When I phoned Head Office about the money that went missing, what d'you think they said?"

They shook their heads.

"They said it was a good thing you stopped them getting away with it. We'd never be able to trace them – they were all in used notes!"

3

SAY IT WITH FLOWERS

Alastair and Arthur – well, to be honest, Alastair mostly – were going over the manager's offer with little enthusiasm as they waited in the luxurious surroundings of the foyer in Whites Hotel for Mr Morrissey to arrive.

As Alastair tried to ease the unaccustomed stiff collar around his neck, he remarked bitterly, "Ten shillings a month. What sort of measly rise do you call that when he's celebrating in a place like this? When I think I had £20,000 in my hands, I could throw up."

"If young George hadn't arrived in the nick of time, you might have had twenty years to think about it – sewing up mail bags," Arthur punctured his dreams brutally. His earlier feelings of almost hero worship for Alastair had undergone a somewhat rapid change after recent events.

"Ye-es," he agreed pensively. "He did manage to turn up trumps though, didn't he?" He glanced around the splendour of the Whites Hotel foyer. "That reminds me, where is George? He'd better put a shift on – he'll miss out on his steak if he's not careful. And old Morrissey's late. Wonder what's holding him up?"

"He's probably found you out. I expect Head Office has checked on your story and they've got the police on to you," Arthur said nastily. "Anyway, you haven't told me how you managed to get Head Office to offer him that promotion."

"Oh that – it was dead easy," Alastair said airily. "All I did was write a letter praising him to the skies and got all the staff and the local tradesmen to sign it. They lapped it up."

"Let's hope the police believe it as well when they check on that break-in story of yours."

"Nonsense, you're worrying about nothing – who's that?" he broke off, clutching Arthur. "Wait, don't look now," he implored, losing his air of complacency.

Arthur shook his hand off. "How do you expect me to answer if I can't see who it is?"

"Use this," Alastair said out of the corner of his mouth and slid something out of his pocket.

Arthur looked at it wonderingly. It was a small mirror from a woman's handbag.

"What am I supposed to do with this?"

"Pretend you've got something in your eye. Quickly, man, he's coming this way! Don't let him see us!" he moaned in deep suffering.

Mercifully, before Arthur had a chance to make a fool of himself, he heard a voice behind him. "Can I have a word with the manager?"

It was the policeman, Detective Sergeant Bird. He walked right past and started talking to the receptionist in an undertone.

Alastair wiped his forehead and agonised. "What's he doing here?"

"How do I know?" Arthur said crossly, stuffing the mirror in his friend's top pocket. "Probably checking up on you."

"Don't let him hear you," Alastair hissed, leading them both away from the danger zone while beaming at everyone around him. A passing elderly lady peered at him and recoiled at the intensity of his smile.

"Ah, there he is," Arthur breathed thankfully. "It's old Morrissey at last. Here we are!" He waved a hand to attract attention.

"Not so loud!" begged Alastair. "Oh, gosh!" he remembered. "We didn't get him anything for his farewell. Quick, slip out and buy some wine or flowers or something. Hurry up, don't keep him waiting."

His friend looked at him pityingly. "What with? I only had enough to get my suit cleaned in time – and some of that came out of next month's salary."

"Don't bother me with the sordid details. Go and say hello to Morrissey while I think of something," Alastair ordered, his thoughts already elsewhere as he gazed speculatively at a party entering the foyer. The hotel manager was ushering in a large, expensively dressed lady, followed by a retinue of servants carrying boxes and hand luggage.

Alastair's eyes suddenly lit up as the hotel manager presented her with a large floral arrangement and he disappeared abruptly, leaving his friend to entertain Morrissey.

"Ah, Conway, there you are." Their portly host arrived, glancing around and nodding to several acquaintances. "All by yourself? I thought I caught sight of Stringer just now. Is he here somewhere?"

"He's just coming," Arthur began nervously, seeing the manager glance automatically at his watch. After their small talk was exhausted, their host began to fidget and frown.

"Where is he?" fretted Morrissey. "You certain he's got the right time?"

"I've just been speaking to him. He's here somewhere." Arthur tried his best to soothe him while he thought up a convenient excuse. Luckily, he was saved from any further embarrassment by the sight of George appearing at the entrance.

"Good heavens," he cried involuntarily, watching the weird figure weaving his way towards them, stopping everyone in their tracks. Gone was his threadbare butcher's apron and in its place a highly colourful attire that could only be described as rather unusual.

The manager blenched. "He's not dining with us, is he?" He looked around with a hunted expression. "Where's Stringer – he'll know what to do."

In answer to his prayers, there was a shout at the other end of the hotel entrance, and Alastair rushed across and handed over a bouquet to the startled bank manager.

"What, what's this? You shouldn't have. Where did you get these?"

A flustered member of the staff hurried across the foyer and appealed to the receptionist. "Has anyone seen Madame Irena's bouquet?"

Morrissey looked at the flowers, slightly dazed, and thrust them at George. "Here, you'd better take them. Hold them in front of you, for heaven's sake." *So nobody can see you*, was the unspoken thought hovering on his lips.

Taking in the situation at a glance, Alastair flinched and herded them over to the desk, looking like a man from MI6 on an undercover operation.

"Have you got a table in a private room – for four?" he asked out of the corner of his mouth.

The head waiter blinked and tried to keep his eyes off George. "Certainly, sir. Step this way."

Morrissey took a deep breath and followed, leaving Alastair and Arthur to bring up the rear, doing their best to shield the other guests from the mind-boggling sight of George. Arthur looked behind nervously, expecting the ominous figure of

Detective Sergeant Bird to materialise around the corner at any minute, but luckily, the corridor was empty.

As soon as they had arranged themselves around the table, George found himself edged out and was forced to take the seat at the other end. He stuck it for a short while but soon bounced back.

"Ay up," he cried, "there's a mouse under the table."

"Don't be silly," said Morrissey uneasily, peering underneath the tablecloth to make sure. Instinctively, the others took a quick look to reassure him. When they straightened up, they found George bouncing up and down in the empty seat next to Morrissey.

"Ha, that fooled you." He leaned over eagerly. "You'll get me in, won't you, Mr Morrissey?"

The manager drew back nervously. "Get you in where?"

"In the local Chamber of Trade, of course. D'you know what, they turned me down last time I asked. Just because I do deliveries. Isn't fair, is it?"

"No, I mean... Alastair!" Morrissey appealed.

Promptly, Alastair shot out of his chair and escorted George back to his seat, whispering in his ear.

Morrissey wiped his face. "Be sure I will look into it, er, George. Now, where was I?" It took half a bottle of champagne to settle his nerves, and after the headwaiter found him a pair of dark glasses so he couldn't see George any more, he began to relax a little.

"Gentlemen, I can't wait to take on my new job," he enthused after a shaky start, as if practising his maiden speech to the directors on his first day at Head Office, "as Assistant General Manager." He tried out the title again, hardly able to believe his luck. "Mind you, it's about time they realised my potential. I'll show them what they've been missing all these years. New ideas and a modern approach, that's what they need. They won't know what's hit them." Then he came down to earth and confided, "I'll be directly in charge of tightening up security at all the branches, you'll be glad to know. That should impress them."

Alastair gave a visible start at the news and Morrissey chuckled.

"I thought that might interest you after that little trouble you had. We don't want any repetition, do we?" He slapped Alastair on the back. "That was a great job you did. Think of all the money you saved the bank – what an achievement to look back on, eh?"

Alastair laughed hollowly.

"I don't mind telling you lads after all we've been through together. Believe me, I'm going to make sure it never happens at this branch again, or any other. You know how?"

Doing his imitation of a Red Indian brave, Alastair moistened his lips. "How?"

"I shouldn't really mention this; it's very hush-hush. Oh, perhaps a little bit more, if you insist." He held out his glass hopefully at one of the bottles that seemed to float towards him.

"No, no, you shouldn't have... just one more, then. I don't often have this chance to relax with all the work I do."

Alastair raised his eyebrows. "No, of course not, sir. We quite understand. You were saying?"

"D'you know, it reminds me of the time I was taken here when my predecessor retired. You didn't know old Busby, did you. He kept us on our toes all right. No Saturday morning sloping off for us, you know. By golly, a real stickler for tradition was Busby – one of the old school. Not many of that type left these days..." He gazed owlishly into his glass, thinking back over old times. "Many's the occasion he caught me at it, doing what he thought I shouldn't, even at the slightest thing. What a tyrant... I mean, what a masterly reputation he had. Bless his old heart – dead now, of course. D'you know, that reminds me about the time I nearly got caught with his secretary when I thought he was out looking after a client – now what was her name... Judy or something? She was a real smasher – nothing like these skinny little types you get around these days, she was something to remember. Now, where was I?" He was about to launch in a flood of reminiscences when Alastair interrupted hastily.

"Good old days indeed, sir. Have another drop." Alastair tilted the bottle encouragingly.

"Good heavens, no more. You'll have everyone thinking I'm a regular tippler. That would never do." He blinked, trying to remember where he was. "Right, where was I? Oh yes," he took another mouthful and chuckled again, "this new replacement manager I've been trying to tell you about, he's just the man to stop that nonsense, I can tell you. No, really, oh, if you insist..." He tilted his glass back and hiccupped. "This is just between the six of us, you understand?"

"Yes, of course, sir," promised Alastair, holding out the bottle temptingly.

What a waste, Arthur thought mesmerised, watching the champagne being tilted liberally into Morrissey's glass.

"Good, because it mustn't go any further. Oh, is that all for me? Now, what was I saying?"

"About the new manager..." prompted Alastair.

"Ah, yes. His name's MacDougal, and he's a tough-looking character. Don't mind telling you – he frightened me a little. Still, that's not surprising under the circumstances, is it?"

Alastair seemed struck dumb, so Arthur ventured. "Why's that, sir?"

Leaning forward, Morrissey smiled happily. "He would do, wouldn't he, when he's from the S.A.S. But keep it under your hat, mind, it's all very ..."

"Hush-hush?"

"The very words I was going to say." He swayed and nodded

off briefly.

George stopped chewing for a second and interrupted excitedly. "I know what SAS means – 'steak and sausages'!"

"Something like that," Arthur said hurriedly. "George, you've missed a bit of steak."

"Ta," said George gratefully, then finished up by licking the plate.

"Sorry, Mr Morrissey." Arthur raised his voice, seeing Alastair's blank look. "Is that something to do with ENSA?"

The manager came to and tut-tutted in a pained sort of way as he sometimes had occasion to do when a customer came up with a flimsy excuse for not paying off an overdraft.

"SAS stands for Special Air Services," he said importantly, pronouncing the words with difficulty. "It's one of those new crack fighting units they set up in the war to drop men behind enemy lines in the desert."

"And he's taking over as manager?" Alastair gulped.

"Yes, I've told him all about you, and he's looking forward to meeting you. You two'll get on like a house on fire." Morrissey gulped down the remains of his drink. "It's time we had some action around here," he announced and promptly slid off his chair.

4

SOME BIG CHANGES

In the good old days when bank managers were in sole charge of a branch, they saw themselves as ambassadors of the profession, setting an example of stern benevolence backed by a keen business acumen. Sobriety indeed was their hallmark.

Not so with the arrival of the new manager at Fleetgate Bank. As soon as he opened the door, he grasped the door frame above his head and pulled himself up into a gymnastic position and proceeded to swing his legs backwards and forwards energetically before lowering himself again.

"There," he said after finishing with a quick burst of running on the spot. "That's what I want to see you doing every morning. It'll make you fighting fit and able to repel any marauders, you mark my words." He glanced around at the slowly slackening jaws, and noting their reactions, his voice hardened in a no-nonsense parade ground manner.

"In case you haven't heard, I'm the new manager from now on, and I'm here to stay," he said, dispelling any lingering hopes that it was all a hideous dream. "My name is Rory MacDougal. For your information, there's going to be some big changes around here. The war in the trenches may be over, but as far as you're concerned, it has only just begun. You play it my way, and everything will be swinging. Otherwise..."

In the hushed silence that followed, the plaintive voice of Symmonds, the first cashier, was heard.

"Is the circus come to town?"

The new manager gave him a withering look. "Yon wee laddie will have a lot to learn. Now then," he said as he gestured for them to line up in front of him. "No time like the present. Ready? Arms by the side. At the command 'one,' arms outstretched above the head then swinging down and back, commence!"

While one or two of the staff made various feeble attempts to follow his actions, the rest just gaped at him stupidly, unable to take it all in. As a result, the manager's hair seemed to bristle at the lack of co-operation, and his eyes turned a fierce green colour as if he were trying to instil discipline into a bunch of raw recruits.

"Ye have no idea, do you. Listen, when I was in the desert facing Rommel with no water or food and fifty miles from base, what do you think I did?"

Arthur watched, fascinated. The unrelenting bulldozer onslaught sounded convincing, but there was something intangible about the way their new manager was behaving that didn't ring true, like an actor who hadn't quite learned his lines. As he was trying to work it all out, the manager nodded at him fiercely. "You, speak up, laddie."

Taken off guard, Arthur stammered and said the first thing that came into his head, "Er, you gave up?"

"No," he said sharply after one or two sniggers in the background. "I didna give up – sir! I did my exercises while the desert sun was blazing down on me. Then I walked – not back – but forward, straight through the enemy lines until I pinpointed their positions and called up an airstrike. So, you see how vital a simple exercise can be. And looking at you lot, I ha' me doubts if you could manage to crawl ten yards."

Showing the first signs of exhaustion, the first cashier lowered his arms and panted, "Can I stop now? It's time for our coffee break."

"Not yet, not yet." The manager broke off, exasperated. "Who's that, now?"

At the click of the latch counter, everyone turned with relief to welcome whoever it was. It turned out to be the chief clerk back from sick leave.

Relieved at the interruption, Alastair rushed forward eagerly and overdid the introductions.

"This is our new manager, Mr MacDougal, Mr Jenkins. He was just telling us of his new plans for the branch," he added. He turned ingratiatingly to the manager. "You haven't met our chief clerk, have you, sir? This is Mr Jenkins. He looks after us like a Dutch uncle and keeps up the good old traditions, don't you, sir," he added appealingly.

"Thank you, Stringer," said MacDougal shortly. "I think I can manage the rest myself. Good morning, Mr Jenkins. I hear you've been away sick. Better now, I hope."

Jenkins raised his eyebrows at the unexpected praise from Alastair. "Still a little wheezy, I'm afraid. But glad to be back."

"Good. Then I'll continue. I was just explaining to the staff that things are going to be a little different around here from now on."

"May I suggest," interrupted the chief clerk tactfully, after a quick glance around and sensing the feelings about him, "we are due to open the doors in ten minutes. Perhaps we may be allowed to go into your plans later on, after close of business. Meanwhile, it is customary for the new manager to look over the ledgers – the staff take great care to keep them in good order. If I can bring these into your office..."

"Not now – I'm not interested," snapped MacDougal rudely.

"As far as I'm concerned those ledgers of yours are a thing of the past – they belong on the scrap heap. We're not wasting any more valuable time pushing quill pens across a page, gathering dust. This is the new age of technology, as you are about to discover."

Arthur glanced at Alastair, mystified, and Symmonds clutched at the chief clerk's sleeve.

"What did he say about the ledgers, Arnold?"

But Jenkins did not hear. He was staring at the new manager in dawning horror. "Do away with the ledgers?" he said faintly. "But-but...how..."

"No time for that now, we're already late as it is." MacDougal looked at his watch crossly, ignoring the fact that he was largely responsible for the delay. "Hurry up, we must get the cash out. Who's got the keys?"

Jenkins pulled himself together and turned to the first cashier. "Symmonds and myself. I'll just get mine out."

Seeing Arthur's anguished look, Alastair stepped forward smoothly. "If I might explain, sir. Shortly before Mr Morrissey left, he decided to promote Conrad here as one of the two keyholders because so many of the staff were away sick."

"You mean, Conway?" managed Jenkins in amazement. He thought he'd heard everything up to that point, but this new blow made him quiver like a leaf in a gale-force wind.

Alastair added hastily, correcting himself. "It was only meant to be a temporary arrangement, sir. Conway under-stands that."

Arthur looked at him coldly, making a mental note to have a strong word or two with him later on.

"Right," said MacDougal, giving a cursory glance. "Give them back to the chief clerk, Conway, and we'll get going. Come along, Symmonds, what's the matter with you?"

"Sorry, sir. I'm still a bit puffed."

"Oh, for heaven's sake, hand them over to me. You're not in a fit state to go anywhere." And with that, he stalked off.

After casting an apologetic look at his first cashier, Jenkins threw up his hands and followed, leaving an embarrassed silence behind.

Bewildered, Symmonds asked plaintively, "Whatever's the matter with the man?" Seeing how upset Arthur was, he placed a hand on his shoulder. "Don't take it to heart, my boy. As for me, I haven't much longer to go anyway." He brushed the cigarette ash off his waistcoat, adding to the liberal collection of stains that had accumulated, a sad reminder of the unkempt state of his clothes since his wife's death.

"But you're just at the threshold of your career," he encouraged, blinking a moist eye. "There'll be another opportunity, you'll see. Perhaps sooner than you think."

"I don't mind," Arthur said awkwardly. "I'll be leaving next year to do my national service anyway." Then he blurted out, "I can't understand him. Anyone would think he doesn't want to make any friends."

"People like that don't think, but he won't last," Symmonds added with foresight.

"What makes you say that?" Arthur was taken aback by his air of certainty.

"You mark my words," was all he would say.

When the manager reappeared, he had the staff running around like scalded cats the rest of the afternoon, and even the second cashier had to stay awake. Life was so hectic that it wasn't until much later on that Arthur managed to have a word with Alastair, who was leaning, panting, against the filing cabinet, his expression weary.

"Do you know, he had me running down to the strong room a dozen times to see how fast it could be done."

"What on earth for?"

"Just testing, he said." Alastair groaned. "There's no pleasing that man."

"But why?"

"Can't imagine, old lad," he said, straightening up with an effort. "All I did was to tell him about how I – er we," he amended, seeing Arthur's expression, "saved the bank from being robbed. And he kept on asking me questions about the strong room keys." He puffed up his chest indignantly. "Gosh, anyone would think we were the villains the way he was going on."

"They certainly would," Arthur agreed drily. "That reminds me, what was all that about me looking after the keys on a temporary basis? You know darn well the manager meant it as a promotion."

"Ah, well..." he stalled. Then his face brightened. "Look out, old Symmonds is calling about something. Sounds important. Must dash..."

But Arthur didn't hear a word he was saying. He was looking over his shoulder at the girl standing next to the beckoning first cashier, and his heart immediately started thumping. *Did I say 'girl,'* he asked himself, searching for an adequate description. He should have said 'goddess,' and the next minute, he found himself at her side, blushing, unaware as to how he got there. "Yes?" he said breathlessly. "C-can I help you?"

Symmonds looked over his spectacles with a twinkle. "This young lady has an appointment with Mr MacDougal, the manager. Would you be so good as to take her to the waiting room, Mr Conway, and see if he is free?"

In a dream, Arthur ushered her into the little cubby hole, laughingly called the waiting room, and after receiving a brief smile of thanks, he reeled away to inform the manager.

"Wow!" was Alastair's reaction when he heard the news. "Who was that dish?"

"Never mind that," Arthur said crossly, annoyed at his familiarity. "What was all that about a 'temporary basis'?"

"It was, er, all in the interests of higher management strategy," Alastair began, edging sideways. Then, seeing his friend's expression, he admitted shamelessly, "Look, I had to say that. It was the perfect opportunity to score some Brownie points and improve my position. I might never get another chance."

"You mean you were sucking up to the manager?"

"Well, if you must put it like that." Alastair dusted an invisible speck of dust off his sleeve. "Some would say investing for the future, perhaps. Anyway, you wouldn't have lasted long with old MacDougal."

"That's not the point."

"What are you going on about – you'll be off to do your national service next year." He sighed. "Lucky devil."

"What's lucky about it?" Arthur stopped, surprised at his words. "Why, aren't you?"

"Dicky heart, old lad." His face assumed a pious look of injured sadness. "We don't all get the same breaks."

The news caught his friend unprepared. "Oh, I'm sorry. I didn't know…"

"Very useful, that wheeze," he added happily, forgetting his pose. "Do you know, Conrad old man, it takes them in every time. It was either that or the feet. Depends whether they want to check me out or not at the medical," he mused. "Feet might be better, of course. It would get me off any drill."

Arthur gave him a scathing look and was just about to retort when the manager's door opened and MacDougal called out. "Mr Jenkins, call the staff in."

They all trooped in, anxious to learn what changes the new manager had in store for them. To Arthur's delight and astonishment, he saw that the girl he ushered in earlier was still there, seated by his desk.

"All here? Good. This won't take long. As I mentioned

earlier, we are going to move out of the dark ages of banking into a new progressive age and adopt the modern technology now being used by all the forward-looking financial centres in London." He glanced around sternly. "Time we pressed on. From now on we're no longer going to rely on old-fashioned manual ledgers using quill pens." He paused for a laugh, but receiving none, his lips tightened and he went on grimly, "We're changing over to the latest accounting systems using electronic equipment."

"But think of all the upheaval," protested the chief clerk aghast, shaken to the core at the prospect. "It will take months to implement. We haven't got the resources for a major change of this nature. It's sheer madness," he burst out, years of caution and discipline thrown to the wind.

MacDougal jutted his chin out. "Are ye questioning my judgement?"

"No, no," said Jenkins, agitated. "But think of the practical side. How are we going to make it work?"

"I've looked into this very carefully," said MacDougal. "My expert tells me that it will only take a matter of weeks to install and have it up and running. Isn't that right, young lady?" He turned to the girl Arthur had been watching in a sort of mental haze and devotion all through the discussion.

"So I understand, Mr MacDougal," she agreed politely. "It's just a matter of examining the existing ledger system and seeing how efficiently the information can be transferred. I imagine it will be quite easy to operate once you get used to it."

"Exactly. I'm sorry, this is Miss Young. She is going to show you how to use the new equipment when it arrives," the manager announced curtly. "See that she is shown where everything is, Mr Jenkins. Perhaps you will look after her while I explain the rest of the details to the staff."

Words of protest hovered on the chief clerk's lips. "Very well, sir," he said at last, a note of rebellion in his voice, "If you will follow me, Miss Young," and left the room looking very upset.

The manager sat down at his desk and relaxed as if he had survived an unexpected battlefield encounter relatively unscathed. He glanced up and seemed to notice who were in front of him for the first time.

"Now then, you two – Stringer and Conrad, isn't it?"

Alastair agreed fervently that was indeed so.

Slightly sickened by his obsequious manner, Arthur spoke out firmly. "Conway, actually."

He waved his hand irritably. "Conway, right. Now I don't know how you're going to fit in to this new set-up. You'll both be off next year on your national service, won't you."

Arthur said yes, but Alastair put on a well-rehearsed act.

"Much as I would dearly love to, sir, the doc tells me I'll be turned down," he said regretfully. "It's the old ticker, I'm afraid." He went on manfully, "But I expect I could just about manage the new system instead." His eyes gleamed. "Provided we can work out a mutually agreeable rate, taking into account current safety practices, and working on new machinery in old and restricted premises and the poor lighting, and bearing in mind union considerations."

MacDougal's eyes narrowed at this. He appeared to be mentally re-assessing Alastair's value in a completely different light. "Well, now, that may not be necessary." He consulted some papers in front of him. "Let me see. Our chief cashier is due to retire soon, and what with all the expansion we're expecting with the new equipment, we could probably do with a reserve cashier." He eyed Alastair reflectively and took note of the eager expression. "Have you had any experience of till work?"

"No problem," lied Alastair convincingly. "Never happier than working on the counter."

"And what about you, Conway? Think you could learn how

to work one of these new," he studied his notes again to refresh his memory, "electronic wizards?"

Arthur hesitated, taken aback at the offer.

"Miss Young would teach you how to operate it," he added casually. "I expect she will be with us for several weeks." He nodded at the immediate wide grin of acceptance on the faces before him.

"Good." He pencilled a tick on a sheet of paper. "That seems to take care of that. I can see we understand each other very well. I think that is all." He got up. "Unless you have any further questions?"

But they were already at the door, grinning like a couple of Cheshire cats. Outside, Alastair did a gleeful war dance, seemingly unworried about the state of his heart.

"Wow! How about that? Did you see the crafty way I handled him? You just wait – I'll show them," he crowed. "Before you know where you are, I'll be taking over as first cashier." Then he looked around guiltily at being caught out and rushed off, calling out, "Mr Symmonds, I've got some great news. Guess who's going to help you on the counter, you lucky old thing."

Arthur watched him, shaking his head. Only Alastair could have got away with a trick like that. He was so engrossed that when a soft voice behind him spoke, he nearly jumped out of his skin.

"May I ask you a favour, Mr Conway?" He turned and goggled at Miss Young.

"Of course – anything you like," he assured her devotedly.

"My manager asked me to come here at rather short notice, I'm afraid, and I haven't had time to arrange any accommodation. I don't suppose you know anywhere I can stay?" Her voice had such a wistful entreaty it would have turned a heart of stone.

Arthur had a sudden flash of inspiration. "My landlady has

a spare room. She told me one of our lodgers is moving out."
He hesitated and had sudden misgivings. "Mind you, it may not
be your cup of tea. It just happens to be very handy for me," he
finished lamely.

She stuck her chin out resolutely at the challenge, and his
heart turned over. "I'm sure it will suit me as well, in that case."
Then she apologised. "That is, if you wouldn't mind showing
me – it's only for a few weeks."

"Only?" he beamed at her idiotically. The prospect filled
him with wild delight. For the rest of the day, he was treading
on a cloud, hardly conscious of anything he was doing and
blissfully unaware of the knowing asides from the rest of the
staff.

When the time came to leave, he insisted on carrying her
shoulder bag all the way to his digs, despite her polite protests,
and felt ten foot tall as he swung along beside her. After a few
words with Mrs Musgrove, the landlady, she left her shoulder
bag in the hall and said she would see him later with the rest of
her belongings.

"Fine," he enthused. "I'll give you a hand if you like."

"I don't think Ben would take kindly to that." She smiled
nervously.

His smile froze. "Ben?"

She leaned up and gave him a quick peck on the cheek.
"Yes, I know you'll like him though, despite his funny ways.
Thank you so much for all your help. Bye!"

Arthur sat through supper hardly saying a word to anyone,
his heart torn by her reference to someone called Ben, then
smiling blissfully at the memory of that darting kiss, full of
fragrance. Percy, one of the lodgers, who had been at the
receiving end of most of his glum looks that evening, caught
the full blast of his soppy grin and it unnerved him so much he
made an excuse and left the table.

"Cat got your tongue?" quipped Mrs Musgrove suspiciously

as she plonked a soggy dish of sponge pudding on the table. "What have you got to say about me potage a la Penge this time? Nothing good, I'll warrant."

"No, it was fine, Mrs M," Arthur told her dreamily, "just out of this world."

"Eh?" She stood there amazed for a moment, then stuck a serving spoon in the sponge pudding to cover her unease. "Well, get stuck into that then." She was so taken aback she waylaid the old Colonel in the corner and whispered in agitation. "Is he all right? I've never heard anyone say they liked it before." She looked back and worried. "I should keep an eye on him if I were you, Colonel. He may be sickening for something."

Her fears were confirmed when Arthur pushed his chair back soon after and announced to the room in general, "I think I'll go for a stroll before turning in. It's such a glorious evening."

"What's the matter with the man? It's perishing cold outside and just starting to rain. He's gone out without a thing on."

As Arthur turned to wave reassuringly to the row of inquisitive faces at the window, he got knocked sideways by a huge bounding shape that hurtled past and disappeared inside to be greeted by a medley of startled shouts and cries.

"Oh dear, was that my Ben who did that?" Miss Young appeared beside him and looked apologetically at his mud bespattered clothes. She helped him to his feet and attempted to brush off some of the large paw marks. "He is such a naughty boy sometimes."

Arthur looked up groggily. "Did you say, Ben – a dog?" A load of anguish rolled off him, and he forgot all about the imprint of the spiked railings down his back in the sudden relief that engulfed him.

"I can see he likes you," she said. "He doesn't do that to everybody."

"I'm so glad," he said weakly. "He's a bit big, isn't he?" He cocked his head on one side. "I say, it's gone a little quiet in there all of a sudden."

"Perhaps they're watching television?"

"No," Arthur said with sudden foreboding. "I think we'd better go and find out."

Inside, all they could hear were a few snuffling noises and a whimper or two. Drawn by the muffled sounds, they left her belongings in the hall entrance and crept along the hallway to the television room where the strange noises seemed to be coming from.

Miss Young looked worried. "That sounds like Ben. I hope he's all right." She flung the door open, and Arthur hung back, half fearing what might be awaiting them on the other side.

"Ben, you naughty boy!" Miss Young was wagging a finger anxiously at the massive hound as it tried to get at a seething mass under the settee. "Put that nice man down!"

Arthur thought she was talking about the Colonel, who enjoyed boring the lodgers every evening with his tales of tiger hunting. He had just slipped off the lamp standard and was sitting half astride the dog, fervently wishing he was back pig-sticking at the foot of the Himalayas.

At the sound of her voice, the mountainous heap of fur raised a head sheepishly, and shaking off the Colonel as if he were nothing more than a troublesome fly, bounded over towards her, licking her all over. A row of heads peered fearfully over the back of the settee, and Percy, one of the other lodgers with a nervous twitch, got up from behind the television set and pretended to adjust the controls.

"Get that monstrosity out of here!" roared the panic-stricken voice of Mrs Musgrove, battling to get the coalscuttle off her head. "Is that animal yours, Miss Young?"

"What a good thing I didn't have my elephant gun handy," panted the Colonel, eyeing the animal nervously from a safe distance. "I might have slaughtered the brute."

"I was hoping you would let me keep him in my room," ventured Miss Young smiling tentatively. "He's really very friendly when you get to know him."

"So I see," said Mrs M scornfully, trying to scrub the coal dust off her face. "Well, there's only one thing I have to say to you, young lady, and that is – get him out of here. Now!"

"But…" attempted Miss Young. "Can't we talk it over?"

"Out!"

"If I paid you an extra something for your trouble…" Miss Young smiled winningly.

"Yes, can't we come to some arrangement, Mrs M?" Arthur butted in anxiously, seeing all his plans going up in smoke.

"Not even for you, Mr Conway." Mrs Musgrave was emphatic. "I wouldn't have that animal in my house for a million pounds, that I wouldn't. I'm sorry, I'll have to ask you to find another room elsewhere, Miss Young." Just to make sure her new lodger was under no illusion, she pointed to the door. "I'll show you out." She swept out, and Miss Young followed reluctantly, trailing Ben behind her.

"Good riddance," sniffed the Colonel, retrieving his tie from the back of his neck. "We don't want people like that around. Good old Mrs M, I knew she wouldn't stand any nonsense."

"Quite so," agreed Percy, looking vastly relieved.

The feeling of mutual self-congratulation was still hanging in the air a few minutes later when Mrs Musgrove flung the door open and reappeared, her face cracking into a smile as if her long-awaited gravy boat had just come in, her whole bearing that of someone ready to break into a song and dance routine at the drop of a hat.

"Miss Young and I have come to a little understanding," she began, directing a roguish look at her newly admitted tenant. "I shan't say any more about that naughty little dog of hers for the moment…"

"That little what?" snorted the Colonel.

"...on the assurance that he will stay in her room and not cause any more little upsets to any of our tenants."

"Little upsets?" echoed the Colonel dazedly, like an ageing straight man caught on the wrong foot in a vaudeville act.

"Yes," smiled Mrs M archly. "Miss Young has convinced me of her good intentions,"

her hand strayed to the bulging wallet in her pocket to reassure herself on that point, and another rare smile broke out, "and I feel amply rewarded by her sincere efforts to make amends. So, we'll say no more about it." With a final look of benediction laced with authority, she swept out again, with the firm resolve to ease the burden weighing down her wallet at the nearest bank safe deposit and call in at the pub immediately afterwards for a celebratory drink on the strength of it.

Miss Young was equally discreet when Arthur tackled her later about it. "Mrs Musgrove's such a dear when you get to know her, isn't she?"

Arthur dropped some of her books he was helping her with, in an attempt to reconcile this new rosy picture of his landlady with the formidable character he thought he knew.

"D'you think so?" he said doubtfully. Then, seeing the glowing look she aimed at him, he basked in the warmth. "Of course," he agreed heartily. "We all think she's... er... quite exceptional." Feeling the phrase might sound inadequate, he added, "She just needs drawing out more," thinking a thirty-ton extraction plant might fit the bill.

"Exactly." She paused and brushed a tendril of hair back and confessed, "I expect that extra money I paid her might have helped a little." Then she gave a pleading look. "But money isn't everything, is it? I don't know what I'd do without my Ben. Like you have your friend, Alastair."

Arthur grappled with this entirely new concept of his relationship and his mind boggled.

"Tell me about this robbery of yours," she added, carefully

ignoring his guilty start, and went on to prod the details out gently until the tale unfolded. "It sounds odd that this should happen when the manager was away, doesn't it?"

Arthur gulped and made some ineffectual noises, and she went on to ask some more offhand questions about Alastair that began to make him quite jealous and uneasy at the same time. As if noticing his reaction, she glanced at her watch and smiled. "Good heavens, is that the time? I'd no idea. Just when I need to make an early start tomorrow in case some of the new equipment arrives. Golly, why is there always so much to do?"

Taking the hint, he said goodnight, getting her to promise to give him a call if she needed anything.

"Thank you so much for all your help – may I call you, Arthur? – I do appreciate it." She held up her face tentatively for a kiss on the cheek, and he stumbled back to his room, reliving every moment of it.

In the early hours, he heard a muffled cry and sat up in bed, his heart thudding. Grabbing a dressing gown, he groped his way along the corridor and saw with alarm that a light was showing under her door and there were frantic movements going on inside. As he got closer, the door was flung open, and Miss Young fell into his arms.

"Oh!" she gasped, then recognising him, clutched his arm. "There's something under my bed, Arthur. I can't bear to look."

"Take it easy," he soothed. "I'll see to it. You stay here." Advancing into the room with more of a show of courage than he felt, he steeled himself and peered under the bed. To his relief all he could make out was Mrs M's tabby cat huddled in the corner hissing and the great bulk of Mis Young's dog taking up an unnaturally cautious position on the other side of the room.

"I expect it was frightened of Ben," he explained. Then he straightened up and was immediately struck dumb by a beautiful vision of Miss Young in a transparent flimsy nightdress that didn't leave much to the imagination.

"Poor little pussy," she cooed with some embarrassment, drawing her neckline together, causing her contours to stand out even more prominently.

He tried not to look at the rest of her and made his excuses, feeling painfully shy all of a sudden.

"Thank you once again, Arthur." She smiled up at him. "You're my great knight in shining armour."

"Okay," he mumbled. "I'll say goodnight then, Miss Young."

"Call me Jenny," she said softly, making up her mind. "If I need your help again, I'll know where to come, won't I?"

For what seemed like hours, he lay tossing and turning on his narrow bed, going over in his mind that last remark of Jenny's. Was she being polite, or did her voice hold out a hint of a promise? As he lay there, he felt a sudden draught from the door and heard a soft padding approach across the threadbare carpet. Then there was an apologetic cough, and an electric thrill ran through him. He half-raised himself and turned back the bedclothes, calling out hopefully. "Jenny? Is it really you?"

The next minute there was a joyful "Woof,", and an enormous weight sprang onto the bed and fell on top of him with a resounding crash and started licking his face. After that, the bed collapsed under him, and he passed out.

5

STRANGE ITEMS OF EQUIPMENT

It was the odd whistling noise that woke him in the early hours of the morning. He managed to extricate an arm from the enormous shape that seemed to be weighing him down and, glancing at his watch, made out with bleary eyes that it was coming up to five o'clock. Turning over with an effort, he came face to face with a great shaggy mass of hair, a tuft of which lifted every now and then to mark another round of whistling.

"Get off, Ben." He tried to get to a more comfortable position, but his visitor just settled himself down more firmly, nestling up to him with a sigh of contentment. As the minutes ticked by, he couldn't say what effect the shifting weight had, but he only knew that it resulted in a sudden and urgent need to visit the loo.

"For Pete's sake, get off – move!" he cried out without thinking. But Ben kept on whistling contentedly and gently snorting into his face.

By then he was getting frantic and started shouting when, to his horror, he heard a door open cautiously and a head appeared.

"Is everything all right, Arthur?"

He looked up feverishly and caught sight of Jenny, standing in the doorway, looking half-awake and anxious.

"No, no. I-I was just trying to..." then finding he had to do something quickly, he blurted out. "I need to get to the bathroom...to clean my teeth."

She laughed to add to his confusion. "What a funny time to think of that...oh," she said quickly, taking in the situation. "Of course, it's my Ben, how did he get in here? You naughty boy – let me help. Come on, Ben."

But despite her entreaties, her dog refused to move.

"I know, "she added brightly, "he probably needs to do his wee-wees. I'll take him down the corridor and find somewhere. Come on, this way, Ben..." She caught hold of him and half-dragging him off the bed, pulled him still protesting towards the door.

As soon as the door closed, Arthur was out of bed in a flash and dived into the bathroom to relieve his feelings. At length, he staggered back mopping his face before shakily climbing back into the warmth of his bed.

Hearing a confused babble of voices breaking out down the corridor, he pulled the blankets over his ears to escape the angry exchanges that followed. After a while, the noise appeared to die down, and hearing a patter of feet outside and a discreet tap on the door, he lifted his head and called out sleepily, "Who's there?"

"It's me – Jenny. Are you awake?"

"Ye-es," he yawned, pretending he had just woken up. "Did I hear something a little while ago?"

"Yes," she said, trying not to giggle. "Some of the other guests were a little disturbed at seeing Ben..."

He stuffed the sheet in his mouth to stop his immediate retort. "Really?" he said instead, trying to sound surprised.

"Yes," her voice trembled. "He thought it was the back door, but it turned out to be the Colonel's."

Arthur couldn't think of anything to top that. "I can imagine."

"I just thought you might like to know. I hope you can get back to sleep, Arthur. Sorry you were troubled."

"Not at all. Goodnight, Jenny." He turned over, blissfully visualising what might have taken place. He tried to get back to sleep but soon gave up, instead deciding to escape the inevitable recriminations from the other guests following the previous night's mix-up, intending to leave for the office before the others came down for breakfast. Someone else must have had the same idea, for just as he emerged from his room, he came face to face with Jenny, tiptoeing out and leading a reluctant Ben behind her.

They grinned sheepishly at each other, deciding the events from earlier were better left unsaid. As they approached the end of the corridor, they were just beginning to congratulate themselves when a door opened and the Colonel appeared, a towel wrapped around his neck, humming to himself and wearing a smug look as if he'd beaten them to it.

At the sight of his fellow lodgers and remembrance of his terrifying experience in the early hours, he gulped as if his worst nightmare had come to haunt him and dashed off in a mad panic, tripping over his towel and disappearing with a howl down the stairs.

"Oh dear, was that because of Ben?" Jenny asked innocently.

But Arthur was already in pursuit, anxious to find out what had happened. When Jenny caught him up, he was bending over the distraught wreck of the Colonel, helping him up and trying to calm him down before the other guests found out.

"Keep him off!" cried the Colonel, catching sight of Ben approaching with a welcoming "woof."

"Don't worry," Arthur said hastily, making up his mind on the spur of the moment, "we're just popping out for our breakfast. We'll leave you in charge."

Before the Colonel could mumble a reply, he took hold of Jenny and led her to the nearest cafe around the corner. Assuming he had been invited, Ben took up a prominent position at the table and resting his paws on one of the chairs gazed pointedly at the food going past.

Seizing the opportunity, Arthur asked awkwardly, "This is all very well, but what are we going to do with Ben at the office?"

The question didn't seem to worry Jenny, and he was beginning to wonder what weight she had behind her from Head Office. "Oh, he'll be all right, won't you, sweetheart?"

Arthur thought for a breathless moment that she was including himself in her remarks and went weak at the knees. But her follow up remark was so obviously directed at Ben that it left him feeling deflated.

"I tell you what," she went on with a confident smile, "we'll find you a cosy little corner where you can curl up, and nobody will know you're there, will they sweetie?"

The thought of Ben being content to stay hidden out of sight for very long left Arthur at a loss for words. He just nodded and averted his gaze, making the best of a bad job and trying to look on the bright side.

After slipping the waitress a hefty tip for keeping Ben happy with a bowlful of treats and sitting back with a cup of coffee after a sketchy breakfast, he said hopefully, "Well, it can't get any worse than that upset with the Colonel, I suppose." How little he knew.

When they arrived at the bank, they noticed a large removal van outside and a driver getting out and checking his list. Inside, Arthur heard with misgiving that their new manager was already at work, shouting commands at the staff in his attempts to get them fighting fit, as he put it. As they made their way in, they nearly collided with the Chief Clerk who backed into them, trying to avoid joining in a weary line jogging around the office, followed by the new manager snapping at their heels.

"Get a move on, what's the matter with you? It's almost time to open up and look at you, you miserable lot. Mind out, you idiot!"

His remark came too late to stop a truck being wheeled in through the entrance. Unable to see ahead, with his head tucked down behind a pile of equipment, the driver added to the confusion by colliding head-on, ploughing into the line-up and ending up with figures flying in all directions.

As if that was not enough, Ben decided it was time to join in and playfully jumped at the driver, knocking him sideways in the truck and scattering half the equipment onto the floor.

"Get that blasted animal out of here!" yelled the manager, looking around furiously.

"You naughty boy, Ben," apologised Jenny guiltily. "It's all my fault, I'm afraid."

"Oh, it's you, Miss Young." The manager subsided after an effort. "You do know that's all your new equipment you've nearly ruined?"

"I'm awfully sorry," Jenny apologised again. "We had a little difficulty finding somewhere suitable for him."

Breathing heavily, MacDougal advanced threateningly towards Ben but, seeing his size, prudently changed his mind, realising the opposition facing him was more formidable than anything he had experienced before in battle. "We'd better put him in the backroom for the time being while we clean this mess up," he temporised. "Now, for Pete's sake, hurry you lot – we open in five minutes!"

Overcome by the news, the first cashier slumped against the counter and passed out, unable to stand the strain. Fearing the worst, Arthur jumped forward and helped him to a chair. While this was going on, Harris the second cashier was about to indulge in his customary mid-morning nap when he woke up to the fact that he would have to take over and move up one.

The only person who derived any pleasure from the unexpected promotion was, of course, Alastair, who couldn't wait to get his hand in the till.

"Whey, this is the life, eh, Conrad?" he cried ecstatically. "Now we are getting somewhere at last."

Arthur had to admit that he was only half-listening. Rejoicing as he was at Alastair's good fortune, he was more interested to hear what was in store for himself.

As if reading Arthur's mind, MacDougal waved Jenny forward. "Now that's sorted out, perhaps we can get down to the serious business. Where's all this new equipment of yours, Miss Young? Are we ready to start training yet?"

Looking a trifle harassed, Jenny smoothed a stray lock back, and his heart went out to her. "Not quite, Mr MacDougal, but we're getting there. I've managed to set up one of the new units, but the others," she took in a deep breath, her voice uncertain, "will need a little attention first. Just a matter of a day or so hopefully." She glanced at Arthur with a look that read 'at least two weeks or more'.

"Good, that's what I want to hear. Now, who will we try out first?" His gaze swept the ranks and came to rest on Arthur. "Conway, of course. The very man. Right then." Taking his acceptance as a matter of course, he went on briskly. "I can safely leave it to you to work out a programme between you." Switching his attention to the state of the office, still in disarray, he was about to go on when he was interrupted by an impassioned protest from the Chief Clerk, witnessing his authority being eroded.

"Sir, this is all most irregular. May I say..."

"Ah, Jenkins, I'd forgotten about you. I'm glad you reminded me." He scratched his chin. "Now we are doing away with all those old-fashioned methods of bookkeeping; I can see we will have to make a few changes in the way we do things around here. Let me see, since you no longer have the responsibility for that side of things, now we have Miss Young to help us, I suggest you look after the foreign exchange for the time being while we decide what to do with you."

"Sir, I protest. This is unheard of. In all the years of my long and faithful service, I've never come across anything like it! Mr Morrissey would never have countenanced such an unwarranted and catastrophic upheaval." His voice began to splutter.

MacDougal gave him a withering look. "In case you haven't noticed, laddie, yon Morrissey is no longer manager here – I am." His voice took on a dangerous turn. "You have, of course, my permission to pass on any concerns you may have to the Head Office." He added smoothly, "No doubt they will take them into consideration while they work out your pension details."

Outraged, Jenkins went pale and stalked out of the office. Although he had nothing more to say, his face spoke volumes.

After he left there was a pregnant silence; then as if unaware of the feelings he had aroused, MacDougal announced his final bombshell. "You do all realise that in order to introduce our new system we will, of course, have to balance the books, so it will mean a late night for us all."

"How late will that be?" asked the second cashier anxiously, waking up in time to hear the last announcement. "I have a most important appointment with my doctor to hear how my mother is after her operation."

"I'm afraid you'll have to delegate that responsibility to others in your family," was the brutal response. "Now, let me make this clear. I expect a hundred percent turn out tonight – and no slacking either." In the stunned silence that followed, he picked up a file and swept out looking, as Alastair remarked afterwards, extremely pleased with himself.

Eventually, Jenkins reappeared with a martyred expression, evidently having second thoughts about taking his complaints any further. Not daring to question his decision, the others listened carefully as he went through the sequence of events that were necessary to balance the books.

After it was all over and they fetched out the ledgers, Alastair whispered, "Thank goodness that's the last time we have to go through all that ledger stuff again – I nearly got cramp entering all that by hand. Kept me awake for ages afterwards just thinking about it."

"I should wait until we've tried out the new method first before we get too carried away," Arthur responded cautiously. "You never know how it will work out."

But Alastair only grinned delightedly. "Don't forget you'll be working it, not me, old lad. All I do is pass it over to you, if you're lucky."

"What do you mean?" he asked suspiciously.

"It's like this," his friend explained brightly. "When old Lady what's her name comes trotting in waving a cheque she wants pay into her account, I make out a slip and pass the lot over to you to enter up on that machine of yours. Get it?"

"When someone shows me how to use it."

"Of course, old lad. We've all got to learn something new now his nibs has dreamed up this new idea of his. I'm looking forward to it." He rubbed his hands in gleeful anticipation.

Arthur was beginning to wonder at the way he put it, whether his friend had some new diabolical scheme for hanging onto to anything that came his way, but prudently kept such thoughts to himself. Before he could comment any further, the manager beckoned them over and ordered them into his office.

As they took a seat, he wasted no time in questioning them

closely on what actually happened at the time of the robbery. Feeling uncomfortable about the whole business, Arthur left Alastair to answer as best he could. Although his friend was put through the mill relentlessly, he couldn't help being impressed at the confident way Alastair went about handling the questions. When he finished, there was a pause while his remarks were being mulled over. Finally, the new manager gave his verdict, and despite Alastair's seemingly polished performance, he didn't sound all that convinced.

"If you want my opinion," he stated flatly, "it all sounds badly organised to me. You shouldn't have fallen for such an obvious con. I know about such things. In future, it will be different around here, I promise you." At the end of the meeting, Arthur was left with the strange feeling that he spoke from personal experience.

"Oh, and while I'm at it," he added casually as they got up, "I might as well check the strong room out to see if everything's as it should be. Let's see, I seem to have Jenkins' keys – who's got the other one?"

Alastair shot forward eagerly to the edge of his seat. "I have, sir. If you remember, you gave them back to Symmonds, and when he had that," he coughed diplomatically, "that...um... turn, he gave them to me for safekeeping."

After a seemingly endless investigation, the manager was apparently satisfied with the state of the strong room and Arthur was allowed to return to his desk, mystified at the apparent motive for their visit. After apologising to the chief clerk for his absence, he was greeted with relief and put on to helping the others with the laborious job of checking what seemed to be an endless stream of entries in the ledgers.

Noting the exhaustion creeping in, the chief clerk called Arthur aside after an hour or so and told him to go to the cafe around the corner and get some sandwiches to keep them going.

As he was about to leave, Alastair muttered out of the corner of his mouth, "What was all that about?"

"You mean the business with the strong room – search me," Arthur replied equally nonplussed. "Must dash, got to get something to eat – tell you about it later."

Alastair grabbed his arm. "That reminds me. While you're at it, you might call in at that hotel where we went with old Morrissey and see if anyone has come across that mirror of mine, I seem to have lost it."

"But I could have sworn I gave it back to you," Arthur began crossly, trying at the same time to grapple with working out what kind of sandwiches he needed to get, when he was interrupted by a breathless voice that sounded like music to his ears, and a soft hand touched his arm.

"I say, do you mind if I come as well?" It was Jenny.

"No, of course, by all means," he assured her, thankful for the delay that had occurred.

"It's just that I need to take Ben back. I can't leave him here all evening while we're working. He needs a break."

"Only too pleased," he gabbled, ignoring the knowing look that Alastair gave him.

As she sped off to fetch Ben, he coughed and mumbled, "Right, mirror and sandwiches, I'll see to that." Before he could say any more, a bounding shape hurtled past, with Jenny hanging on breathlessly behind. Catching her up, he grabbed the lead to help her slow Ben down and thankfully they were able to rest for a brief moment as her dog caught up with an interesting smell and stopped to investigate.

"I'm so glad you were there to help," she gasped thankfully. "He's rather a handful sometimes."

"He is a bit on the large size," Arthur ventured, averting his gaze from the enormous shape as he got up to resume his search for more pleasurable pursuits elsewhere. "How long have you had him?" he asked, using it as an excuse to find out more about her.

"Ever since," she paused while she wrestled with the lead and confessed unexpectedly, "ever since we had that silly family do of ours." Before she could say any more, she shot away, hanging on for dear life.

He waited expectantly, as she went on another ten yards before Ben found another diversion that made him stop for a brief pause. "Not with Ben, of course," she added, searching for some way of explaining it. "We had this... disagreement in the family. It all happened after my mother died, bless her, and my father married again." She sighed. "I was very young at the time. It's hard to explain. He had another daughter, my half-sister." Then in a burst of candour, she said, "I did try, but we never got on very well together. She brought a new boyfriend home she was crazy about, and he turned out to be a bit of a rotter." She grimaced. "We found out he was playing around with half a dozen others at the same time – he even tried it on with me, but I told him to get lost. For some absurd reason, she blamed it all on me afterwards – said it was all my fault. Which is why Ben came along."

He looked mystified, and she laughed. "I'm not explaining this very well, am I?" She tried again. "It all happened when Dad took us for a walk in the park one weekend hoping to patch things up, and some dog came along and jumped up at her when we were in the middle of an argument about the way her boyfriend was treating her. She shouted at him, poor thing, so I had this idea of getting a dog that wouldn't stand for that kind of nonsense, just to teach her a lesson."

"And that's how you found Ben." Arthur eyed the dog in a new light.

"Well, to be truthful, he found me. The pet's home was glad to see him go. It must have cost them a fortune, just to feed him – apart from all his playful habits."

He followed her gaze and nodded agreement at her masterly understatement.

Sensing their lack of attention, Ben bounded back and started jumping up, anxious to get going again.

Freeing himself from his clutches, Arthur got his breath back and patted Ben's head encouragingly. "Yes, I see what you mean. So, I imagine you don't get invited there very often now."

"Not these days, "Jenny admitted sadly. "Our old home's not the same any more, I'm afraid. Dad couldn't stand the bickering in the end, and his wife persuaded him to go back to the States where she was from and start up a new life together, away from it all. He didn't want to leave us and sends us money, from time to time, to make sure we don't go short of anything. It's a shame really when something like that happens. I just had to try to put it behind me, but it upset me and always will, I suppose. Anyway," she shook her head with an effort, "I'm so busy these days, I hardly have the time to see anyone. What about you?" she said, changing the subject.

"Oh, I live in digs at the moment." Explaining, Arthur told her about his aunt and how difficult their relationship had been.

She pressed his arm in sympathy and exclaimed as Ben gave another tug at his lead. "I'm sorry, I seem to be holding you up, just as we were getting to know one another. I know you need to get those sandwiches back to the others; otherwise, they'll all be starving, and it's all my fault."

"Not at all," he apologised. "My fault entirely – keeping you gassing like this. See you later, I hope."

"Of course." Jenny hesitated, then said shakily, "I don't usually go on like that, boring you with all my family history, but talking to you like this has made all the difference. I knew I could trust you. I've never met anyone before who I've really liked." Her face turned pink, and she put out her hand. "I'd better go. Goodbye, Arthur. You're such a dear."

"Me too...." he began to stutter. "I mean, I feel the same. If there's anything I can do – you've only got to ask."

"I'm so glad. You..." her voice was lost as Ben gave a sudden heave and she was off again. "I'll be back... as soon as I get Ben settled," her voice floated back. "Byee."

Arthur waved until she was out of sight, then turned towards the shops reluctantly, still wrapped up in a dream world. After nearly walking into the path of a taxi and getting cursed at, he came out of his mental fog and remembered with a guilty start that he had to call in and enquire at the hotel Alastair had mentioned. If he didn't get hold of that mirror of his, he'd never hear the last of it. As the sign 'Whites Hotel' hove into view, he turned in at the reception and pressed the bell at the desk, hoping they would have the mirror Alastair had mislaid. In the event, he got more than he was bargaining for.

"Yes, sir. How can I help you?"

Arthur turned and goggled at the girl who appeared. For a moment, he was lost for words. As she repeated her request, he took another look to collect his scattered wits.

She tapped a pencil on the desk. "Is there something wrong, sir – you have the right hotel, perhaps?"

"I think so..." he stuttered and gave her another glance of disbelief. For the girl facing him bore a remarkable resemblance to Jenny, who he had left only a few minutes earlier.

6

A BIT OF A HANDFUL

Recoiling with a nervous start at the identical version that faced him, Arthur clumsily upset the flowers on her desk, and she politely helped him to replace them before resuming her seat and raising her eyebrows invitingly. "Well then, how can I help, sir?"

He coughed and made an effort. "I'm sorry... I thought for a moment... excuse me for asking, but um... do you ever get mistaken for anyone else?"

She laughed amusedly. "Not very often, sir... except..." Her face sharpened with interest. "I do sometimes get compared with," she hesitated, "with another member of my family. Why do you ask?"

"It's just that I happen to know someone who looks very much like you..."

He trailed off and tried to change the subject with a weak laugh that sounded like a croak. "But in your job, I expect it happens to you all the time."

"Not very often." She pulled a pad towards her casually. "May I ask who that might be... in case I get asked again?"

Arthur hesitated, wondering if Jenny would mind.

Before he could think up an answer, the receptionist gave an encouraging smile as she dusted the counter with a careless wave. "It wouldn't be one of my relatives, Jenny, by any chance – Jenny Young?"

The expression on his face evidently gave her the answer she was waiting for.

"I thought it might." She adopted a look of sweet sadness. "It seems ages since I saw her last. How is she?"

He mumbled that she was feeling fine.

"Do give her my love."

Before he could think up a suitable reply, she glanced at him half-defiantly and said without thinking, "I suppose she told you I was her wicked half-sister?"

"No, no," he protested. "She just mentioned it in passing. Jenny... I mean, Miss Young, is very busy with her new job – in fact, she tells me that it doesn't leave her much time to keep in contact with all her family and friends, much to her regret." To forestall a protest, he noticed forming on her lips, he added quickly, "On top of all that, she has her hands full looking after her new pet dog."

The mention of Ben seemed to spark off a long-felt sense of grievance. Her smile vanished in a flash, and she seemed to forget both herself and her surroundings. Without warning, she threw her pen down on the desk to express her deep feelings on the subject. "Don't speak to me about that animal." She fixed him with an accusing eye as if it was all his fault. "It should be locked up in a zoo; she only bought it to get back at me." The thought of it evidently released a store of pent up jealousy and she burst out furiously, losing any element of restraint, everything pouring out of her in a wave. "She's always resented me, just because Father decided to marry again. Then she had the cheek to try to steal my boyfriend... the cow!"

Hastily remembering her position, she added with an

apologetic smile, "I meant cow-slip, of course. How silly of me. She was always fond of those flowers – how sweet."

Arthur held up his hand to stop her saying any more. Already, one or two heads were poking around the entrance at the disturbance.

"Now, now, I'm sure it's not like that. She's never said anything against you, believe me. I would have known."

"Really, sir?" She smiled archly, and he found himself going red in the face at the emphasis she placed on his remark. After eyeing him with a speculative look, she calmed down slightly, forcing a smile. "I'm sorry, sir, I was forgetting myself."

Arthur made some soothing noises. "I quite understand. I'm sure most families have their little upsets from time to time; it's only natural."

"Quite, sir." She straightened up, patted her hair. "Let me see, you were going to tell me how I can be of service."

"Oh yes." He tried to remember why he was there. Then it all came back to him. "That's right, a colleague at the office thinks he may have left a small hand mirror when he was here recently. Can you tell me whether it has been handed in?"

"A hand mirror?" Her brow became furrowed as she went through the motions of recollecting, while her mind appeared to be treasuring up his recent remarks.

"It was when my manager, or should I say, former manager, Mr Morrissey, booked a room here for a celebration quite recently," he prompted.

"One moment, sir." She consulted a bookings diary. "Yes, I see." Then she busied herself, searching in a drawer. "No, we don't seem to have anything like that at the moment."

"Oh." Arthur mentally cursed Alastair to himself. "He's probably got it all wrong. Well, never mind, I'll let him know. I expect it will turn up. Thanks anyway." He turned to go.

"Wait, sir. If anything turns up, we will let you know. But," she smiled winningly, "perhaps you could let me know where I can get in touch with you for the record. You never know, it might very well turn up before you know where you are."

"Of course." Arthur gave her his name and office address and, once more, started to leave.

"And just in case we want to contact you out of hours," she appealed engagingly, "I'm sure your friend would like to hear, as soon as we have any news?"

"Ah, yes, good thinking." He mopped his head and obliged, anxious to get away, and a gleam of satisfaction flitted across her face.

Freed for any further questions, he hurried away not appreciating the value of his information, only intent on finding the nearest store where he could lay his hands on those confounded sandwiches he was sent out to purchase in the first place.

When he got back loaded with food, he thought would keep everyone happy, he was immediately pounced on by Alastair who couldn't wait to get started. "Where have you been?" he accused between mouthfuls. "Here am I working myself to the bone while you've been gallivanting about, no doubt finishing off some enormous spread without a thought of us slaving away... that reminds me, where's that mirror of mine you were supposed to get?"

Arthur broke the news to him, and he was highly indignant. "You mean to say you've been halfway around London trying out all the snack bars you can find while we've been working our socks off, and you haven't even got the one thing I sent you out for?"

While he was talking, Arthur debated whether to tell him about his meeting with Jenny's half-sister, then thought better of it. "Look who's talking." He averted his gaze at the sight of Alastair's face smeared with a mixture of salad cream and sticky bread crumbs. "You're worse than George. You've already helped yourself to half my share – and where's that ham sandwich of mine I had just now? That was my last one."

"Oh, was that yours?" Alastair looked innocently surprised. "Never mind, you can always scrounge another one-off old Jenkins. He's probably got some leftover – I don't suppose he'll feel like eating any, the way things are going."

"Why, have the others snaffled them all? That reminds me, he hasn't paid me for them yet."

"You'll be lucky – you'd better get in there quick while there's still a chance. I doubt if he'll be around much longer. Haven't you heard?" He lowered his voice as he looked around cautiously. "Old McDougal has it in for him – I wouldn't be surprised if he's got someone ready to fill his boots."

Arthur felt bewildered. "What's happening? It was all quite peaceful when I left, apart from everyone hard at it, balancing the books."

"You should have been here," he said mysteriously.

"What do you mean? He was all right when I showed him over the strong room earlier on."

"Yes, and why did he want to go over it again, when I'd already been, that's what I'd like to know? Why did he want you to do it a second time? What did he ask you, for Pete's sake, that made any difference?"

Arthur went back over the questions he'd been asked and the answers he gave.

When he finished, Alastair looked fogged. "Why, that's exactly what he asked me." After a pause, he said slowly, "The only thing I can think of is that he wanted a second look around to memorise everything, but why?"

Arthur shook his head. "There must be a good reason – he's not that stupid."

They looked at each other and Alastair glanced up and warned, "Look out, it's old Jenkins. Now's your chance to get your expenses."

"Ah, Conway, my boy – about those sandwiches."

"There you are," whispered Alastair. "I told you so. He's hasn't got it – I bet he's had the push."

Arthur nerved himself up for whatever was coming with apprehension.

To his surprise, Jenkins placed a friendly arm around his shoulders and boomed, "Now then, how much do I owe you?"

After he'd recovered, he told Jenkins nervously, and the chief clerk thrust a note in his hand. "There you are my boy, that should cover it I would imagine, and a bit over for your troubles." Noting Arthur's half-open mouth, he said unexpectedly, "Excellent sandwiches by the way." He heaved a sigh at the sight of all the equipment piled up around us. "Let's hope the new system is just as good – though I doubt it."

The sight of him standing there looking rather sad and lonely at the thought of what the changes would bring made Arthur feel sorry for him.

Pulling himself together, Jenkins announced with an effort, "Well, that's all finished – I expect it's the last one I'll have to sit through." He clapped his hands to gain attention. "Right, you can pack up and go home now everyone, it's all over. Thank you for all your splendid efforts. We'll just have to see what tomorrow brings. You'd better turn up at the usual time to find out. Goodnight."

"What did he mean 'see what tomorrow brings'?" Arthur asked mystified, "And where's Jenny – I mean, Miss Young?"

"Ah, that's another thing. When she finally got back, he nearly blew his top for her being so late."

"She was probably having a job settling Ben down," Arthur said defensively. "He's a big boy."

"You can say that again," agreed Alastair pensively. "More the size of Ben Nevis. But on top of all that, she found that none of the new machines were working because that dog of hers had upset half the equipment all over the place. You should have been here to see it. He was livid."

"So, what's happening tomorrow?"

Alastair shrugged. "He sent her off with a flea in her ear and told her to find out from the suppliers what they can do about it, and pronto."

"And has she?"

A smile played over his lips at the thought of how the setback would affect him. "Don't ask me, old lad. I doubt it; we'll just to wait and see. Meanwhile," he slid off his seat gratefully, "I'm off for some shut-eye." He added gleefully, "If we don't get those machines working tomorrow, we'll have to shut up shop. Cross your fingers – it'll probably get us another lie in. Heave ho – it's a hard life."

Ignoring his remarks as typical, Arthur was more concerned about Jenny and how she had been getting on. Wasting no more time, he set off back to his digs, anxious to find out if she was back and hoping she had managed to get what she wanted. When he arrived, there was no sign of her. He bounded up the stairs to her room only to find a note pinned on her door. It read, 'Dear Arthur, if you get back first, could you be a dear and look after Ben? I may be held up for a while. Hope I won't be too long, Jenny.'

Making use of the key she had left behind, he opened the door cautiously, only to be knocked over by a familiar bounding shape that proceeded to launch himself at his victim and lick him all over. Fighting him off, Arthur distracted his attention by filling his bowl with water. After watching him lap up vast quantities, he prudently decided to walk him downstairs for what Jenny called, his 'wee-wees.' Hearing the rest of the lodgers making the most of their meagre supper, he crept past the dining room and let Ben out.

By the time he'd allowed the dog to explore all the smells he was interested in, and after fighting his way back upstairs heaving a reluctant Ben behind him, he was feeling slightly exhausted. Not content with his drinking session, Ben proceeded to pull him towards a cupboard in the corner which he scratched at pointedly. After wolfing down half a tin of dog food Arthur found inside, followed by a supply of biscuits, he looked up as if to enquire what was next.

Arthur groaned to himself. He could see it was going to be one of those nights. In the hour or so that followed, Ben gambolled around the room, hauling him along behind him while he decided what he could get up to next. By this time, Arthur, feeling the strain and mopping his forehead, called on Ben to give up and take a breather, feeling just about all in. He was about to collapse and give up caring when there was a light footstep outside, and Jenny entered and threw herself at Ben with a cry of delight.

"Darling, has that nice man been looking after you?" After cuddling the great brute and crooning over him, she noticed Arthur's somewhat dishevelled appearance and rushed over with cries of gratitude. "Oh, Arthur, I am sorry – have you had a lot to deal with? I feel awful about leaving Ben with you all this time."

"No, no." He forced a smile. "Delighted. He's been quite... exceptional."

She looked closely. "Have you had anything to eat?"

He did his best to reassure her. "Yes, I took some sandwiches back to the office – they went down a treat," he said, omitting to mention that Alastair had scoffed most of them.

"Wait a minute." She delved into her bag. "The people who supplied our equipment were so apologetic when they heard about our troubles they insisted I had these sandwiches, after filling me up with masses of food." She pressed them on Arthur and tried to hide a yawn. "Excuse me, they went on so long about how difficult it was going to be replacing our equipment, I was dying to get back and have an early night."

Arthur was immediately concerned and looked at his watch. "I'd no idea what the time was." Tempted by the offer of a snack, he swallowed. "Why don't you get some shut-eye." He hesitated. "If you're sure about these," as she pressed the sandwiches on him, "I'll... em, look after them for you. By the way," he added as he started to leave, "I shouldn't be in a rush tomorrow. I think everything's in a bit of a mess at the office."

"I'll be there as usual and face the music." Jenny forced a smile. "Thank you so much for your help, Arthur, you are a dear. I don't know what I'd have done without you." She held her face up for a kiss.

Without thinking, he kissed her cheek and was about to forget himself in a mad moment by clasping her in his arms, when he was attacked from the rear by Ben who evidently thought it was his turn to be petted. They broke off with a giggle from Jenny.

"I think he's trying to tell you something." She yawned again helplessly, then apologised and confessed. "Oh dear, it's awful. I can't wait to get into bed." She reached up impulsively and kissed him breathlessly. "Oh, Arthur, you'd better go before I forget myself."

Swallowing, he stepped back and squeezed her hand. "You're not the only one." Taking in her tired expression, he accepted the sandwiches she offered and, tenderly pushing a stray lock back behind her ear, quietly left.

It was not until he was in bed and about to go to sleep that he remembered he hadn't told her anything about meeting her half-sister.

Next morning as Jenny joined him, she seemed preoccupied as she slipped on Ben's collar and they set off for the office. Then apologising, she looked up appealingly. "Don't tell me last night was just a lovely dream, Arthur dear."

"No, it really happened." He squeezed her hand, intoxicated by the memory of her kiss.

She halted and turned up her face expectantly. "Remind me what it was like... oh my goodness, help," she called back as Ben dragged her off in a gallop, feeling he had been ignored.

Catching her up, Arthur grabbed hold of her and plucking up courage while he had the opportunity held her close. "Jenny, I've never felt like this with anyone anywhere before," he stammered.

"Well, I'm here now," she invited shyly.

Making the most of her invitation, he put all his feelings into a long and satisfying kiss.

"Oh Arthur, that was wonderful," she began, then stirred and drew back apologetically. "If only this had happened before all that trouble at the office."

"What does all that matter?" he whooped, all his nervous tension gone at the thought that she cared. He felt so uplifted, he wheeled her around in a wild celebratory mood. Any troubles at the office meant nothing to him at that moment. So great was his excitement that Ben decided to join in, getting both of them entangled in his lead, and Jenny fell about laughing at the mix-up in spite of herself.

Sobering up, Jenny pulled at his arm. "You don't understand, darling."

"Did you say, 'darling'?" he asked tenderly, cupping her face in his hand.

"Yes, but listen, darling, this is serious. Mr McDougal is furious with me – you should have heard him."

He shook her gently. "You don't want to worry about that. He's been having a go at everyone, so I'm told. Our chief clerk is even getting it in the neck, so Alastair tells me."

"You don't understand," she repeated insistently. "I had a call to ring my office this morning. He's been complaining to my boss about the new equipment we've supplied."

"But he'll calm down surely – he'll be so delighted to get

your new machines in, he can't wait to see them working in place of the ledgers."

"Oh, you don't know, do you?" She tugged at the lead miserably. "Apparently, after we left last night, he went back and tried the new machines himself and couldn't manage to make either of them work. I knew that some of them had been put out of action, but I hoped we'd get by with what were left. He says it's all because of Ben and it's all my fault – he was furious."

"But your people will be able to replace them, surely?"

She shook her head. "It's not that easy. The ones we've been given are the latest on the market. They've only just been developed, and my boss tells me it'll take ages to sort them out."

Arthur tried to reassure her. "They can't blame it on you after all that business of rushing the staff around on those mad exercises of his – no wonder it got out of control."

Jenny couldn't be persuaded. "It isn't as if I'd been there very long. It was my first job there, and now it's all gone up in smoke – all because of Ben here." She threw her arms around the dog. "My darling Ben." She gave an anguished cry of help. "What am I going to do with him. I can't take him to the office – he'll throw a fit if he sees Ben again. What am I going to do?" she repeated. "Don't tell me. You think I'm mad to get such an enormous animal – just because I wanted to teach Doris a lesson."

Caught off-guard, Arthur asked bewildered, "Who's Doris?"

"My half-sister, didn't I tell you. She'd be laughing her head off if she heard about this."

"Oh, ah," he came up with lamely. "There's no need for her know, is there?" instantly deciding not to reveal about his meeting.

"That doesn't answer my question, does it? What shall I do with Ben – I can't bear to part with him."

He had a sudden inspiration. "I know, I'll have a word with Alastair – he's full of bright ideas."

"Oh, do you think so – that would be marvellous if he could." She took a quick, doubtful look at Ben. "He's a bit of a handful if you don't know him – are you sure?"

"Of course," Arthur said hurriedly, trying not to imagine the prospect. "He'll do anything for me – he'd better," he added, remembering all the nightmare events that the man in question had put him through in the past.

Being practical, Jenny thought about it. "I tell you what, I'll wait outside while you go and have a word with your friend."

So that was how they left it. As they approached the entrance, they noticed a queue beginning to form outside, waiting for the doors to open. When some of the onlookers caught sight of Ben, they edged away nervously.

"Now's your chance," whispered Jenny as the crowd opened up.

Slipping inside, Arthur approached the counter and saw the rest of the staff were already lined up, waiting for the signal.

"Good morning, sir," Alastair said automatically still checking his till, then looked up crossly when he realised who it was. "Where have you been? I've been looking all over for you."

"Can't explain now, what's happening?"

Alastair pulled a face. "That's what we'd like to know." He leaned forward confidentially, seeing the coast was clear. "There was I expecting the old man to shut up shop so we could all go home when he turned up and told us to wait until we had a meeting – we're still waiting."

"Look, could you do me a favour – or rather, Miss Young, actually," Arthur added before his friend could protest. "She's got to get in to have a go at the new machines to get the system running – but she needs someone to look after Ben," he added hopefully.

Alastair's eyes bulged at the prospect, seeing his chance of taking the day off vanishing, coupled with the ghastly thought of what it would mean, coping with Ben.

"You're joking!" He jumped back and nearly upset the contents of his till. "You must be stark raving. As if I would consider such a daft idea."

"She's willing to pay you."

"Ah." His eyes gleamed at the opportunity. "It would cost you – how much?"

Arthur named what he thought might be a reasonable figure, but the other snorted.

"You can double that, for a start." He had another think. "No, make it treble, before I'd even consider it."

Expecting such a response, Arthur said, "Wait here, I'll go and ask her."

Alastair heaved a sigh moodily. "As if we've got any choice."

After reporting back and finding Jenny surrounded help-lessly by a hostile crowd, she blinked and accepted his demands with a rueful shake of the head. Relieved, Arthur returned to find Alastair bursting with unexpected news.

"You'll never guess, he's shut up shop and given us the day off. No, not you though," he added gleefully. "He wants Jenny to have another go at getting those machines working again, it's her last chance – and you've got to stay behind and help her."

"Right, I thought you'd say that," Arthur said nastily, forti-fied by the thought of helping Jenny, "and your little playmate is waiting outside."

Alastair's eager smile vanished as he emerged behind the counter nervously. Catching sight of Ben bounding towards him, he quaked. "What did I say, I must have been out of my mind." The rest of his words were lost as he disappeared under Ben's hurtling shape and got licked all over.

"He is sweet looking after him," beamed Jenny, turning up to hear the verdict. "I see Ben's taken to him already."

"Ye-es," Arthur said doubtfully. "I'm not sure he feels the same."

"Right, I'm so pleased that's sorted." She held his hand trustingly. "Now, we'll have to see what the manager has to say – I'm glad I've got you to give me support, Arthur."

From what one could tell, it turned out that the manager had quite a lot he would like to say, but he restrained himself with a supreme effort, aware of the presence of a witness.

"Miss Young," he said weightily, "as you might imagine, I'm not at all happy at the way our plans are progressing after such a promising start, but now that you are here, no doubt you will be able to assure me that the new equipment will up and running shortly, if not sooner, ye ken." He measured his words majestically, like an elder minister of the glen rebuking a newly acquired member of his closely-knit community.

"I'm so sorry about all the trouble you've had," Jenny said, smiling bravely, "but I'm sure we will have it running again as soon as I can have a chance to look at it, and I've got Mr Conway here to help me."

"I have my doots, Miss Young," he replied, giving Arthur a frosty glance as if dismissing the idea out of hand. "I'll have you know I've already tried without success. But seeing as you're the expert, no doot you will have better luck. I'll be in my office, if and when you have anything to report." And with that he stalked off, barely concealing a snort of derision.

"Right then, Arthur," said Jenny doing her best to sound confident. "Let's go and see what can be done."

Arriving at the back of the office where the new equipment had been installed, Arthur groaned inwardly at the shambles that confronted them.

"What a mess," he gasped involuntarily.

"Don't look too closely, darling. Now, what have we got here?" She pulled off a cover and winced at the battered equipment exposed. "One thing at a time." She tried the keyboard experimentally. "Well, that seems to be working, let's see if..." She pressed the bar alongside. "No, that's had it, I'm afraid." She tried to remain practical. "I'll see if the other one is any better." Getting the same results, she glanced up desperately. "Those are the only units I hoped might still have some life in them, and neither of them are any good – what am I going to do? Oh, Arthur."

He was about to make some fatuous consoling remark when the phone next to them rang.

Jenny pulled herself together. "I'd better answer it...Yes?" she said distractedly. "Who is that?" She glanced up. "It's my office." Pressing the receiver to her ear, she raised her voice. "I can just about hear you – who's speaking? Oh, it's George. Listen," she took a deep breath and broke the news, "they're not working... yes, both of them." She went into technical details. "I've tried that...What was that? I didn't quite catch... you've what?" she whooped. She almost dropped the phone in her excitement. "You've had another delivery? I don't believe it!" She held a hand over the receiver and turned up a glowing face. "We're saved!"

"Steady on, what's happened?" Arthur was so infected by her mood he nearly snatched the receiver away to find out more.

Jenny covered the receiver and steadied her voice. "It's true, oh, Arthur, I can't believe it. It's the second batch we were expecting, and they got held up. They've turned up out of the blue – that means we can start using them right away. Yes, I'll come as soon as I can." Replacing the phone, she added, sobering up, "Mind you, we will still be operating at less than half-strength, but at least we'll have something."

"When will they be able to deliver?" Arthur interrupted tactfully, bringing her down to earth.

"That's what I need to find out. I'd better go and break the news to the manager before he blows a gasket."

Emerging from the office after a brief consultation, she rushed over anxiously. "Arthur dear, do you think you could be an angel and look after Ben for me – I must get up there right away and arrange a delivery. Do you mind awfully? I don't know how long I'll be – I might be late back. I daren't leave it to my office to organise; the manager is making me personally responsible. He wants those units back here tomorrow, or else..."

"Don't worry." He calmed her down. "You go and see to that equipment and forget about everything else. I'll see to Ben." He crossed his fingers mentally. "He'll be as right as rain."

7

AN UNEXPECTED VISITOR

As he saw her off in a cab, he was beginning to feel in a more light-hearted frame of mind, relieved at the sudden turn of events. It looked as if all their immediate problems were going to be sorted out. He glanced up and down as he stood there and patted the doorway affectionately, thinking how lucky he was to find his dream girlfriend at last, and all coming about through working in the bank... with the help of that crazy friend of his who had made it all possible. Then it all came back to him. He had a sudden twinge of guilt and wondered uneasily what had happened to Alastair and that dog of hers she idolised.

He reluctantly surfaced from the romantic fog that surrounded him, and his eye caught signs of a disturbance along the street. He thought he might as well find out what all the fuss was about as something to pass the time, while he was waiting for Alastair to return.

Heading in that direction, it occurred to him that, however much he trusted the idiot, he was certainly taking his time getting back. He suddenly had an uneasy feeling about what might be waiting around the corner, and with increasing foreboding, he neared the scene to be confronted with the sight of Ben sitting astride the bonnet of a taxi, resisting all efforts of the driver and Alastair to dislodge him. By now, they were beginning to attract a growing crowd of onlookers who were taking no notice of a constable doing his best to move them along.

"Help," screamed Alastair catching sight of his friend, as some of the crowd started pulling at him, thinking he was harming the dog. "Get them off, Arthur."

He duly obliged, but when he tried to get hold of Ben's lead, he found himself being frustrated by a burly onlooker who evidently disagreed strongly with his efforts and proceeded to give him the elbow in no uncertain manner.

"Here, watch it mate," he warned, "keep your hands off, nothing to do with you. This 'ere' berk is asking for trouble, the way he's going about it. Some people didn't deserve to 'ave animals the way they treat them."

He was joined by a beaky-looking housewife wielding an umbrella which she flourished energetically. "Yus, push off, mate. This ain't your fight. Go somewhere else. We're trying to save an h'animal here. It ought not to be allowed. I see'd it all."

"Wot was that?" She was joined by a newspaper boy, no doubt looking for a new headline. "Wot's up, guv? Any bodies lying around?"

"And you can push off as well," was all the beaky housewife would spare. "Go and do your homework and leave it to the grown-ups to deal with."

"It's all right for you lot, what about me bleeding cab?" complained the driver bitterly. "I've got a customer waiting, and I can't move. Hi, officer, give us a hand, mate."

Answering the call, a harassed constable appeared. "What's all this? Who does this animal belong to?"

Seeing salvation at hand, Alastair pointed at his saviour, between bouts of fighting off the lady with the umbrella.

"There he is – Arthur, do something!" he yelled, pointing. Instantly, all eyes switched in his direction, and he became a focus of attention.

"Ho," said the constable, getting out his notebook. "Can I have your details, sir?"

Arthur told him tersely as he wrestled with the lead.

"You do know your h'animal is parked illegally for more than the prescribed limit, sir? I'm afraid I must report you to the authorities. Meanwhile," he eyed the driver formally, "I shall have to give you a ticket for harbouring the said h'animal and causing an obstruction."

"I can't help it," yelped the driver. "I didn't put that ruddy great monstrosity there. Get him off my cab – he's ruining the paintwork."

"And what about the perishing dog – nobody's thinking about him, poor little devil?" called out one of the spectators in a plaintive voice.

"Yus, and keeping him sitting on top of the flaming bonnet in this kind of weather – it's ruddy inhuman, that's wot it is," cried another.

"Read all about it," cried the newspaper boy, seeing his opportunity.

"'Ere sonny, you'd better scarper – you don't want to get mixed up in the fight."

"Wot fight, can I join in?" said the newspaper boy jumping up and down excitedly.

"This one," said the burly onlooker, aiming a punch at Alastair.

"Throw the book at him, mister – ought not to be allowed." There were indignant murmurs from all sides.

Stung by all the remarks, the constable shifted his position after placing a hand on the bonnet to steady himself against the pressure of the crowd around him, then quickly withdrew it with a muffled oath.

"I should caution the lot of you for causing an obstruction," he complained, sucking his fingers.

Frustrated by the turn of events and finding the bonnet too hot to bear any longer, Alastair decided to make a move, sliding off and jerking at Ben's lead as he did so. Immediately, there was a hostile reaction.

"'Ere, mind the poor dawg."

"You're strangling the blessed thing."

"Let go of the perisher."

"Do summink, Officer, don't just stand there."

"Wait till I get to 'im with me umbrella."

"Watch it, mate, before I paste you one."

Seeing the mood turning ugly, Arthur made the mistake of intervening.

"My friend was only trying to help."

Taking his cue as an encouragement, Alastair gave an extra tug and immediately caused an uproar. A fight broke out, and he disappeared under a sea of waving fists. Arthur staggered back, and after receiving a thump and dabbing at a cut lip, he was dimly aware of a whistle blowing in the vicinity. A few moments later, there were sounds of a siren and screeching brakes, and the crowd started melting away before he passed out.

When he came to, he found himself propped up in a court answering to the law, with a dishevelled Alastair hanging on the rail beside him, facing the unsympathetic eye of a magistrate.

"What are the defendants' names?" he heard the magistrate asking sternly, his eyes boring into them as if already deciding on the severity of the sentence. Arthur looked around in a daze to see who he was talking to and realised with a shock that he meant Alastair and himself.

Waking up with a jerk, Alastair answered automatically, after sifting his memory and coming up with a convenient alias. "Tom Brown, your worship." Before Arthur could collect his wits together, Alastair went on hurriedly, giving him no opportunity to answer. "And my friend here is Albert Smith."

"Really? That name sounds familiar from my school days," the learned magistrate began reflectively, then coughed. "I see you are charged with causing an affray; of encouraging a dangerous animal to trespass on this gentleman's property," nodding towards the taxi driver, "followed by unseemly behaviour amongst other serious offences, including a charge of illegal parking."

At the word 'charge,' there was a crash at the back of the court, and Ben burst through a door, accompanied by two court officials gamely hanging onto his lead.

"Remove that animal," ordered the magistrate, vainly banging his gavel a number of times before he could gain attention. Whilst order was being restored, he found he had been overzealous with his wrist action, and an attendant had to come to his rescue, picking up the shattered remains of his gavel. After the uproar eventually subsided, accompanied by plaintive yelps from Ben, the magistrate straightened his gown, adjusted his wig that had fallen over one eye and tried to compose himself, regally dismissing the interruption. Reinforced with extra guards, Ben finally disappeared with a howl after casting a beseeching glance up at the dock.

Peering over the top of his glasses, his honour addressed the court with a note of self-righteousness. "I get far too many of these cases coming up before me these days, and I am obliged to consider imposing a heavy sentence to make you aware of such disruptive actions. I would be failing in my duty if I didn't."

The two accused held their breath as he shuffled his papers around.

"However," he went on, "in view of the fact that we do not appear to hold details of any previous convictions of either of you on our records," they gulped, "I feel it will be sufficient to impose a summary fine of £10 each and you will be bound over for the next six months. No doubt you will be hearing from the driver of the vehicle in due course. Case dismissed."

As Alastair groaned and waved his arms at Arthur at the verdict, an attendant presented the magistrate with a slip of paper. After a muttered consultation, the magistrate added, "I should have mentioned that there will be a bill before you leave for housing the said animal and keeping him restrained during the case – that will be another £2."

He was about to go through the motions of looking around for his gavel when an attendant whispered in his ear, and he added with a frown, remembering the loss of his trusty hammer. "Oh yes, and other, ahem, administration expenses, making twenty-seven pounds thirteen shillings and sixpence in all. Next case."

Outside, Alastair gave full vent to his outrage. "Twenty-seven quid? That's all my savings gone up the spout, I ask you. After all the time spent looking after that blasted dog and the nightmare he's caused... twenty-seven quid!"

"How did he get up on the taxi's bonnet?" Arthur broke in, anxious to find out what had happened.

"Fat lot of business making any money looking after that blasted dog – he's ruined me," Alastair moaned, brushing aside any questions.

"Don't forget I'm paying half," Arthur reminded him. "How did he get on the bonnet?"

"All because he saw your friend getting into a cab and tried to follow her. That driver wasn't silly – he managed to nip off smartish like before Ben could get aboard – the second one who came along wasn't so lucky."

"That explains it," his friend reasoned thoughtfully. "What an intelligent hound. Never mind," he pointed out helpfully, "you probably won't have to do it again. Miss Young will probably have to find somewhere else to park him during office hours, particularly after that last dust-up at the office, unless," he suggested with a light laugh, "she makes an offer about Ben you can't refuse."

"Never again." Alastair shuddered. "It's the last time I do anything for that hound. "Twenty-seven quid, I ask you! And on top of that, we'll have that blasted cabby chasing us for damages."

"Don't forget the thirteen shillings and sixpence – just as well you didn't give him your real name," Arthur reminded him.

His face brightened for a second. "That's true, particularly after that recent... misunderstanding at the bank." Then he sank in gloom again. "There was I ready to splash out on a night out, and this had to happen."

"What's all that again, 'splash out'?" Arthur asked jokingly. "Have you got a girlfriend tucked up your sleeve I don't know about?"

"No such luck," Alastair said with a pained expression. "Directly I spin them the usual story about 'why don't we go Dutch' when I take them out for a meal, they seem to find one damn silly excuse after another. Women..." he expressed himself at some length.

"It's all right for you," Arthur said unsympathetically. "I've got the job of looking after Ben until Jenny gets back – goodness knows when that will be."

"Rather you than me." Alastair cheered himself up at the thought. "Let's hope she doesn't get hold of any more of those units, then we can take a few more days off."

Not surprisingly, Arthur was feeling a bit pooped when he finally got back to his digs. He was about to sneak up to his room, hoping the sound of the television would help to muffle Ben's entry when the landlady popped her head out of the sitting room and hailed him.

"Oh, there you are, Mr Conway."

He halted, half-expecting her to deliver some sort of ultimatum about Ben when she announced, "I thought you might like to know that you had a young lady asking for you earlier. I was out at the time, but she left a note to say she would be calling back later." She consulted a message. "Her name was a Miss Leeds."

The name meant nothing to Arthur, and he said so.

"Apparently, she asked after Miss Young, and when she heard she'd been delayed, she said she'd look in later in the off chance you might be in. I hope that was all right?"

"Absolutely," he agreed absently, more concerned with getting Ben settled down for the night. Perhaps the unexpected visitor, whoever she was, would only stay a few minutes and allow him to sit down and relax and put the day's events behind him.

He finally got Ben settled and with a sigh of relief sank back into what his landlady proudly described in her leaflet as one of her stylish deluxe armchairs. Ignoring the squeaks and twangs from the bursting upholstery, he pondered about the possible identity of his unexpected visitor. For a ghastly moment, he wondered if she might have something to do with their recent court appearance, then dismissed the notion, reflecting that they had managed to get away with it after passing themselves off, or Alastair had, under assumed names. Then another disturbing thought occurred – supposing she might be a relative of the real Tom Brown?

He struggled to his feet again, setting off another series of squeaks, and decided to treat himself to a drink to help forget about the whole affair. After surviving the stressful events of the day, he felt he deserved one. As he sipped the glass appreciatively, he pondered anew about the visitor's identity, and to bolster his morale refilled his glass from a bottle he'd set aside for a rainy day and for sudden emergencies. If this didn't constitute an emergency, he couldn't think what did.

By the time his landlady called up announcing his visitor, he found to his surprise that he had some difficulty in getting to his feet. Responding to a discreet tap on the door, he heaved himself up and started to weave his way in that direction, only to discover that he had indulged rather too freely.

Straightening himself up, he opened the door and received a shock. For the lady standing there with a polite smile of greeting was none other than the receptionist from Whites Hotel, Jenny's half-sister, Doris.

"Hello, I'm so glad to find you in," she began apologetically, flashing an encouraging smile.

"Not at all," he managed, opening the door. "Come in." He waved a hand politely, finding it difficult to get the words out. "What can I do for you?"

"Thank you," she said, slipping past. Looking around quickly, she said hurriedly, "I'm so sorry to disturb you, but I thought you might like to know that one of our guests handed in a mirror they found and I thought you might be interested in case it turned out to be the one your friend was seeking. I'm sorry, I hope I'm not disturbing anything."

"Not at all," Arthur replied thankfully. "That would be great. Come in and sit down. Can I get you a drink," he offered invitingly, finding he needed one after getting over her surprise announcement. "I'm sure my friend Alastair will be delighted."

"If I may – just a small one." She darted a quick glance around the room. "I'm sorry if I came at the wrong time – are you expecting anyone?"

"Not for some time yet," he confessed, trying to sound cheerful.

As Arthur handed her a glass, he said without thinking, "Jenny won't be back for hours yet. I'm looking after Ben – her pet dog," he explained to cover his slip.

At the mention of Ben, she started and nearly spilt her drink. "He's not here, is he?" she asked nervously.

"No, thank goodness, he's fast asleep. He nearly added 'a good thing too after the dance he's led us,' but prudently kept the knowledge to himself.

After that she began to relax, loosening up a little and telling him about the guest who found the mirror, going on to describe some of the everyday demands of her guests and how she managed to deal with them. "Not that I mind the work, I'm quite happy to stay there... until the right man comes along."

"Come, come, I'm sure that won't be too long – a pretty girl like you," Arthur responded, thinking how much she matched Jenny's good looks.

Her lips tightened. "I doubt it," she said without thinking, "after my past bad luck in that direction, thanks to someone I could mention. Oh no." She covered her glass half-heartedly, then gave way. "Well, perhaps just a little," she added roguishly, allowing her skirt to rise, revealing a generous glimpse of flesh. She crossed the floor and settled down next to him, tipping her glass invitingly. "I don't think we've met before, have we? How long have you known Jenny?"

"Not all that long," he confessed uneasily, trying to edge away.

She snuggled closer. "I mean to say, now we've been introduced so to speak, it might be fun to get to know you better, don't you think?"

Hastily ignoring the invitation, Arthur raised his glass. "Here's to the future then." He waited for her to finish, expecting her to wind up the proceedings and decide it was time to go.

Taking the hint, she struggled to her feet, all in a flutter. "Oh, I don't know what you must think of me, going on so long, I do apologise. I'm so sorry I missed seeing Jenny. Do give her my love." She hesitated. "I wonder if I might have a peep into her room before I go, just as a reminder – you must think what a silly thing to ask, but I would like to see if she has any," she searched for an excuse, "family photographs to remind me of the old days, you know the sort of thing I mean."

"Of course, let me show you." Arthur led the way with her following on tiptoe, half-expecting Ben to wake up and make them welcome.

"How lovely," she enthused, "just as I imagined. Oh, I nearly forgot. I must pop back and leave you that mirror I mentioned."

"Oh, wait, I'll see you back downstairs, the lighting is not so good at this time of night," he began politely.

"No, it won't be necessary," she insisted. "I have a torch – really." As he demurred, she trilled, "You stay here, please." Struck by a sudden thought, she added, "You can't leave Ben in case he wakes up and disturbs everyone – I'm sure Jenny wouldn't like that. Goodnight and thank you so much. I did enjoy our little chat."

"I'll tell Jenny you called. She'll be sorry she missed catching up on all your news."

"Oh, she'll remember all right." She smiled briefly as if the thought amused her.

As he went to see her out, she stopped him hurriedly and pointing at Ben, whispered quickly, "Oh, do look, he's waking up. Don't let him see me. He may think I'm up to something."

While Arthur stayed to make sure, she made a hurried exit, closing the door behind her. Hearing funny noises from Ben's corner, he wavered and sat down and waited. After a while, Ben grunted once or twice and turning over stretched out and went back to sleep again.

He must have dozed off because the next thing he knew someone was gently shaking his arm.

"Oh, you poor thing, have you been waiting up all this time? I'm so sorry I'm so late. Will you ever forgive me?"

He opened a bleary eye and consulted his watch. "Good heavens, it's nearly midnight, I had no idea, is that the time?" He yawned and lurched to his feet, forgetting where he was for the moment.

"Oh, darling, you look all in. Let me help you back to your room. Take my arm; easy does it."

As Arthur let her guide him, stumbling and only half-awake, dimly aware that he had drunk too much in her absence, she babbled on excitedly, "You'll never guess, that nice boss of mine has promised to deliver those new units first thing in the morning."

She opened the door to his room and after helping him in stood there, staring about her almost unbelievingly, trying to take in the shattering evidence laid out in front of her. "What on earth?"

Arthur blinked at the transformation. Instead of his nice neatly made-up bed, the bedclothes were pulled right back as if in a hurry to disclose his pyjamas loosely strewn across the bed, and lying next to them a half-torn chemise as if one of the occupants couldn't wait to strip it off. To top it off, a tray nearby held the remains of a half-empty bottle and a glass smeared with lipstick to complete the picture of what looked like an unashamed evening of endless debauchery.

"Who...what...What has been going on?" She looked at Arthur in shocked surprise and let go of him so that he stumbled and reached out for a chair for support. "Arthur?" Her voice trembled. "What does this mean?"

He goggled speechlessly at the scene. "I've no idea," he

mumbled at last, looking around completely at a loss. "She was only going to fetch that mirror..." he trailed off.

"She?" Jenny drew away, her eyes mesmerised by the chemise. "Are you trying to tell me you had a woman in here... and you never told me?"

"But I didn't, I mean, she wasn't – we were in your room."

"In my room, that makes it worse. Oh, Arthur, and all the time, I trusted you."

"But it wasn't like that," he stammered. "It was all because of Alastair and his blasted mirror. I called in Whites Hotel where he says he lost it, where we had that farewell do, and your sister said she'd look out for it."

"Doris... what did she have to do with it?"

"She was working there."

"Why didn't you tell me this before?"

"I didn't want to worry you about it when you were so involved in that business about your equipment."

"I suppose you welcomed her with open arms," she accused, glancing at the bed and wiping away a tear.

"You don't understand what I've been through," he said wearily. "After finding that idiot Alastair trying to get Ben off that taxi and landing up in court on the strength of it, I was bushed."

"That's no excuse for behaving like you did! What taxi?"

Arthur did his best to explain, but she stamped her foot, outraged. "And that's what happens when I leave Ben in your care? I should have known."

"Be reasonable," he begged her. "When I got back here, I was completely bushed and needed a drink."

"So I see," she said icily, nodding at the half-empty bottle and the state of the rumpled bedclothes. "I should have known if it was anything to do with Doris. I suppose that's when you persuaded her to join you in a disgusting orgy – no doubt she didn't need much persuading." She drew herself up, tight-lipped. "That's the last time I'll ask you to look after my darling Ben or anything else. I never want to see you again." And with that, she burst into tears and rushed out of the room.

As Arthur turned to try to stop her, his foot got caught on the wretched mirror, and he tripped and hit his head on the bedpost, passing out for the second time that day.

8

MOST SOUGHT AFTER BANK

When Arthur came to, he found himself fondly clasping a pillow, half-hoping it might be Jenny, and suffering from such an almighty hangover he thought for a moment a band of the household cavalry were tramping over him in full chorus with studded boots. Resisting the temptation to pull the pillow over his head to muffle the drums, he managed to get to his feet shakily and looking at his watch with bleary eye groaned at the time. Half-past eight, he howled inwardly. He only had half an hour to get to the office. Hastily swallowing a couple of aspirins in a half-tumbler of scotch that went through him like a fiery flame, he hurriedly stuffed the offending chemise out of sight in a drawer and stumbled next door to make sure he hadn't dreamed it all. It was completely empty.

Shattered, he made his way unsteadily downstairs and was about to sneak out when he was waylaid by his landlady who threw up her hands when she saw him.

"Whatever have you done with that nice Miss Young? I thought you were such good friends."

"So did I," he said glumly. "If you'll excuse me, I must fly, I'll be late for work."

Undeterred, she clung to his arm while she appealed to the other lodgers who were hastily gulping a coffee down and getting ready to make a dash for it themselves before getting involved in one of her everlasting cosy chats.

"But I hear she has gone," she wailed, waving her arms inviting support from around her. "We can't allow that, can we everyone?"

She turned back again, missing the vigorous head shaking going on behind her that would have left her in no doubt as to the general census of opinion on the subject.

"And that little sweet dog of hers," she went on determinedly, ignoring the frantic signals aimed in Arthur's direction. "We all loved him, didn't we?" At the mention of Ben at this point, the Colonel had one of his spells and had to be helped to his feet after collapsing.

Taking advantage of the disruption, Arthur made his escape, shaking off her hand and promising over his shoulder that he would have a word with Miss Young at the earliest opportunity.

"Don't forget now," she called out after him. In a wheedling voice, she added, seeing hopes of her newly gained cash flow vanishing over the horizon, "I'm sure we could come to an arrangement, Mr Conway – just between the two of us. What d'you say?"

But he was already halfway out of the door. He was so anxious to get to the office and find out what had happened to Jenny he nearly ran into Stuart, the messenger, at the entrance just as he was about to step out and check up on his paper rounds before starting off his day. Accepting Arthur's apologies, he flicked the ash off his cigar. "If I might advise, sir. I find it easier to put a tie on *after* one does the shirt buttons up. Allow me." While he carefully adjusted the offending article, Arthur danced up and down in protest.

"There, that's better, sir." He stood back. "One must remember the traditions at all times."

"Yes, yes, thank you, Stuart," he said hastily, and dashed past, scanning the counters and beyond, searching for signs of Jenny.

Defeated, he was just standing there wondering what to do next when a hand reached out and grabbed him.

"It's no good searching for your friend – she's been and gone." Alastair looked his friend up and down critically. "What's happened to you – you look as if you've been in a rough house with that dog of hers. Here," he peered closer, "you haven't had a dust-up with her?" Seeing Arthur's glum expression, his face cleared in sympathy. "That accounts for it. No wonder she had the sulks. She's been snapping everyone's head off since she's been here." He shook his head. "I thought you had it made – what went wrong? Come on, you can trust me."

Ignoring the outrageous claim, Arthur heaved a sigh. "It was all because I called in that hotel you mentioned to ask about your blessed mirror and the girl on the counter turned out to be her half-sister."

"Didn't know she had one. Did she find it?"

"No," he admitted wearily. "But I left my address, and she turned up in the evening saying she'd found one."

"Good. So where is it?"

He fished the battered remains out of his pocket and handed it over.

"Here, that's not mine." Alastair pushed it away in disgust. "Looks as if someone's trodden on it. Fat lot of help she was."

"Oh, she helped all right," Arthur said grimly. "She helped by sneaking next door while I was looking after Ben and trashed my bed to make it look as if we'd spent the night there together."

"Ooh, so you're quite the Romeo." Stifling a chortle, Alastair corrected himself hastily. "No, I don't see you in that role some-how. Well, why did she do it?"

"Because... oh, it's a long story. Apparently, they didn't get on ever since she accused Jenny of pinching her boyfriend."

"And did she?"

"No, Jenny's not like that – the boyfriend turned out to be a rotter anyway."

"What was the idea then?"

Arthur thought back over the events. "I can only think she must have been looking for some excuse to get her own back."

"I've got it." Alastair's eyes widened comically. "You mean that when Jenny got back, she thought you and she were..."

"Exactly." Arthur gritted his teeth. "Now, Jenny doesn't want to have anything to do with me."

Alastair whistled. "No wonder she was in and out like a flash. What are you going to do about it?"

His friend shook his head despondently. "You tell me." He had a sudden thought. "She didn't say anything about coming back? She was supposed to be showing me over the new machine."

"You've had that, mate. She's getting someone else to come instead, so I hear." Alastair toyed with his pen and asked casu-ally, "She sounds quite a handful, this sister of hers. What did you say her name is?"

"Doris," he said shortly. "She's a half-sister apparently, her father married again."

"Hmm. I might just call in there myself and enquire." Antic-ipating a suspicious glance, he said quickly. "You never know, she might come up with the real thing this time after you managed to muck it up – I mean, the mirror, of course. What does she look like, this Doris, so's I can recognise her when I see her?"

"She looks exactly like Jenny," Arthur admitted with a sigh.

"Is she now?" His eyes lit up. "Sounds a corker – I mean,

quite an interesting encounter, from what you say. It might be worth investigating. Meanwhile," he said, changing the subject hurriedly, before Arthur could questioned his motives, "I don't know what you're going to do until this new one turns up instead of Jenny – I should go and find out. Old Jenkins might know – he's got nothing to do now he's stuck on foreign exchange. We could always do with a cup of tea," he suggested hopefully, cheering up at the thought.

Following Alastair's advice, he consulted Jenkins who seemed too full of his own problems to be of much help. "Don't ask me, young man. Wish I knew myself. I don't carry any weight around here anymore. You'd better ask the manager – he's the one who thinks he knows all the answers."

His gloomy remarks were interrupted by a young lady bursting into the office and ending up panting at their side. "Excuse me, which one of you is Mr Conway?" she blurted out.

Seeing the state she was in, Arthur did his best to calm her down. "How can I help you?"

She appeared very flustered. "Miss Young asked me to take over and show someone how to operate one of our machines. I'm terribly sorry I'm late. I should have got here ages ago but got held up by the traffic."

"I don't suppose it matters," he reassured her. "We don't seem to have many customers at the moment. By the way, I'm Arthur Conway – the one you're going to help."

She flashed a sigh of relief. "And I'm Nancy Slimsby." She smoothed her dress down apologetically. "I know I don't look like it, with a name like mine. It's all this sitting around that doesn't help very much. Now, where do we start?"

Arthur gave her a friendly smile. He could see he was going to like this friend of Jenny's. She was bouncing around like an eager puppy – just like Ben, he thought, and built on the same robust lines.

"I'm hoping you're going to show me how one of those

machines works before the morning rush starts." Arthur glanced at his watch. "It used to happen before lunchtime when they came and unloaded their takings – but since we had to shut up because of the changeover we've hardly had anyone in here."

"Oh, in that case, we've got plenty of time. Don't worry; I'll deal with them when the time comes. Meanwhile, it won't take me long to show you the ropes. Now if you'll sit by me, I'll go through the routine."

True to her word, Nancy soon introduced Arthur to the mysteries of the new accounting system and before long she had him picking it all up at a satisfying rate, between gusts of laughter as the inevitable mistakes were made. It got so bois-terous that even Alastair was attracted by the noise and saun-tered over to see what was going on.

"Hello, who do we have here?" He tried his usual tricks of giving her one of his over-friendly pats. "Who's this attractive new recruit? Introduce me, old chap, don't keep her all to your-self. You can call me Alastair – what do they call you, good looking?"

Sizing him up, the new supervisor gave him a no-nonsense look. "I'm Nancy – Miss Slimsby to you."

Disregarding her advice, Alastair put his arm around her, but she pushed it away smartly. "And you can keep your hand off me, young man. I'm here to teach Mr Conway. I can see you don't need any teaching, thank you very much."

"Well, well." Alastair disentangled himself. "In that case, I'll leave Miss Slimsby in your good hands, Arthur. Oh, my hat, look out, it's old MacDougal." He straightened up. "Morning, sir."

Casting a quick look around the office, the manager beamed at them all so heartily that Arthur nearly lost his place on the keyboard.

"Everything coming along as planned? Good. I see you're

getting the hang of it already, Conway. At this rate, we'll have to start thinking about getting some more operators in to handle the workload, isn't that so, Miss... um?"

"Slimsby, sir." Nancy stood up respectfully. "Normally, we find you will need at least three or four operators to run the system properly in a branch this size. I am glad to say Mr Conway is proving an excellent pupil, but when the rush builds up, you will need to engage some more staff, I would think."

"Quite right, we must get onto that right away." MacDougal straightened up with the sort of commanding air that Napoleon would have admired. "You may have noticed that some of our regular customers seem to have deserted us pro tem due, ahem, to the unfortunate lapse in getting our new system up and running. But they will be back – mark my words. My ambition is to make this the most sought-after bank in London, and when customers can see what kind of service we can provide, they will be flocking in, I'll see to that. That reminds me, I must have a word with Mr Jenkins and see he gets it organised right away. Meanwhile, carry on the good work."

And with that thought-provoking sentiment, he turned on his heels and left a stunned silence behind.

"The man's raving mad," uttered Alastair, bewildered, after recovering from the shock. "We'll never get that number turning up in a month of Sundays."

"It does sound a bit over-ambitious," agreed Nancy tactfully, looking up at Arthur to see if he agreed.

"Crumbs." He swallowed, wondering what he'd let himself in for. "I hope I can do it justice before any of that kind of rush begins."

"Never mind." Nancy gave him a motherly smile. "I'll look after you, don't fret. Wait here; I'll have a word with my office. They'll know what to do." She bustled off like a girl guide anxious to win her day's brownie points.

Within minutes she was back, beaming all over her face.

"It's all fixed; I can stay on as long as your manager agrees. And I can't see him arguing if he wants to make this the most sought-after bank he's been talking about."

"But two of us won't be enough," Arthur argued, imaging the nightmare of dealing with a long queue of people all wanting to be served at the same time.

"Don't worry; I've already thought about that. My boss is going to have a word with your manager about it. He'll need to get at least one other to help us if he's got any sense."

Overhearing their conversation, Alastair broke in happily, "And if he doesn't, I dare say I could lay my hands on one or two."

"Meanwhile, you can keep your hands to yourself for a start, if you don't mind," said Nany shrugging him off tolerantly.

"Hey ho," sighed Alastair, giving Arthur a wink. "I know when two's company. If you don't want me, I'm sure my customers will always be willing to oblige. Coming, Mr Symmonds."

Shaking her head, Nancy laughed. "Don't take any notice of him, Arthur, you're doing fine."

As the day wore on, he found himself becoming increasingly confident until Nancy exclaimed at one point, "Goodness, at this rate I'll be able to set up my own machine and leave you to it, without any trouble."

Although encouraged by her remarks, at the back of his mind, he kept on wondering what he would say to his landlady when he got back, about not being able to get hold of Jenny. He winced at the thought.

When it was time to go, he mentioned this to Alastair who had solution straight away. "No problem, come and doss down with me, old lad – plenty of room at my place. Besides," he reminded Arthur, "we've still got that whacking great court fine to pay off. If we share digs, it's going to make it much easier."

The idea sounded attractive, but Arthur baulked at the

thought of having to explain it all to Mrs Musgrove face-to-face and be subjected to yet another of her cosy chats.

"Nothing to it," dismissed his friend airily when he mentioned the problem. "Leave a message for her at your digs, that's all you have to do – much easier that way." Seeing Arthur's doubts, he added, "You don't have to go into too much detail – just say your aunt's been taken ill and you've got to stay and look after her. Tell her you'll pick up your things later on – she'll have forgotten about it by then."

"Yes," Arthur said, brightening up. "I never thought of that."

"You see, you can always rely on your old mate. Leave it to me – I'll see to it."

"Would you?" Arthur said gratefully.

It wasn't until he had settled in and had the loan of a spare pair of pyjamas that he learnt just how great a sacrifice Alastair was willing to make. He discovered after a chat with his land-lady that splitting the cost of his rent meant that he was paying most of Alastair's share as well as his own. When he remonstrated about it, his friend was quite unabashed, claiming his landlady had made a mistake.

"As if I'd charge you extra," he said heartily. "She's got it all wrong as usual." He leaned closer, "I blame it on all these pictures she goes to – never been the same since she saw Clark Gable in *Gone with the Wind*. Like some of those customers I've been dealing with." He harked back to a particular grievance that had been troubling him. "I thought this job of being a cashier was going to be dead easy. They didn't tell me they would be using a paying-in book with all that cash they were handing over. That's no use to anyone."

Arthur gaped at him. "That's because it gives them a record of what they pay in, you idiot." He gave an amused chuckle. "You'll be telling me next you were expecting to get a share of it."

"Well, fair's fair," Alastair defended himself. "How do you

think I'm going to pay off that blessed court fine. Twenty-seven quid, I ask you."

"They'll be giving you a stiffer sentence than that, if that's what you were expecting – more like fifty years, without an option," said Arthur dryly.

"Anyway," Alastair cheered up, "I've thought up a much better way than that to drum up some cash."

"Legally, I hope."

"Lord, yes. That's why I asked you to come over to my place – it makes it so much easier. It's a chance to make some real money, at last, all quite legitimate."

"Oh, yes?" Arthur said guardedly.

"Yes, don't bother to get undressed yet, old lad. We're off to try our luck tonight, you and me together."

"What's the plan?" Arthur asked cautiously, fearing the worst, knowing his friend.

"See this old treasure of mine?" Alastair picked up a battered instrument that bore a faint resemblance to a banjo and gazed at it fondly. "This little beauty is going to make our fortune."

"You won't get much for that old thing," Arthur said disparagingly.

"I'm not selling it, you ass. I'm going to entertain them with it."

"You're going to play it?" Arthur stared at it incredulously. "Nobody's going to pay to hear that." He was still repeating this half an hour later when Alastair led him to a spot outside a swanky restaurant in town.

"Ah, but you miss the whole point," Alastair stressed as he sat down and made himself comfortable. "When they hear this, they can't wait to pay up – you'll see."

After strumming a few bars and making a particularly hideous noise, the door to the restaurant sprang open, and a waiter erupted waving his arms frantically. "Go away, mon dieu, you'll frighten the customers away!"

"Spare something for my wife and six kids, guv," pleaded Alastair in an atrocious cockney accent, holding out a begging bowl he had borrowed from his landlady's kitchen.

"It's a wonder your poor wife can stand that sort of racket," snapped the harassed waiter, forgetting his French accent. "Here, take this and vamoose."

He thrust some notes in the bowl and strode off.

"There you are," beamed Alastair, getting up and stretching himself. "It's a doddle. Not bad for starters."

"You mean, you're going to inflict that," Arthur strove to describe the awful sound they'd heard and failed, "on someone elsewhere?"

"Too right, old lad. A few more of these and we'll be sitting pretty."

"In a cell, more likely," Arthur pointed out nastily, "with no remission."

"Nonsense, things are just about to warm up. Now if you would be so good as to take my arm as befitting a poor old gentleman down on his luck as I am, I would be so grateful." He paused as a young couple approached and stopped to consult an address. "Thank you kindly, sir." He doffed his cap.

"There you are," he rejoiced after they passed on. "It works every time, like a charm. Now, where's that other place I was thinking of?" He consulted his notes. "Ah yes, just around the corner."

"You mean, you've done this before?" Arthur gulped horrified, pulling his arm away.

"Yes," Alastair told him happily. "It's a good wheeze. Come on, I can't do this without your help."

As Arthur hesitated, he urged, "You do want to pay that fine off, don't you?"

"There must be another way," he objected nervously. "Supposing someone from the bank recognises us?"

"Don't be daft – in these outfits?"

At the sound of his voice, a couple passing turned and peered at them uncertainly. "Good heavens, it's not young Stringer and Conway from the bank, is it?"

Arthur gulped, and Alastair seemed to turn a pale green under his make-up.

Recovering, he put on a breezy act. "Why, if it isn't Colonel Smythe-Smythe and his good wife, how nice to see you both."

"What on earth are you doing in that outfit," demanded the Colonel in his usual no-nonsense manner.

Caught up in a moment of inspiration, Alastair exclaimed brightly, "It's, um, for the bank fancy dress party, Colonel, didn't you know?" On the crest of a brainwave, he plunged on, "Why, it's all the rage, isn't it, Arthur. My friend's a West End agent – does all my bookings," he explained outrageously, making it up as he went along.

In the end, the Colonel gave up, and waving his stick, he departed, pulling his wife after him, muttering, "Ridiculous nonsense."

"There you are, Arthur, how was that?" Alastair wiped his brow, waiting for applause.

"I think it's time we went home before we get reported," Arthur replied firmly.

Alastair reflected. "Perhaps you're right." Then he clapped his friend on the back.

"Still, it was fun while it lasted, wasn't it. Let's go home and see what we've made."

Drinking a hot cup of tea back at the digs, he spilled the coins and notes across the table in a grand gesture, with satisfaction. "I make that eight quid, all but sixpence – not bad for our first night out."

Arthur shuddered. "If you think I'd go through all that malarkey again, you can count me out – forget it."

Alastair looked at him in hurt surprise. "Is this my old friend Arthur speaking, the one I put forward for the treasured role of keyholder, and who I cheerfully shared my last sandwich with?"

"The role you gave back, you mean – and you pinched my last sandwich, remember?"

Alastair regarded him sorrowfully. "Is that all you can say after all we've been through together?"

"Let's put it this way, "Arthur answered bluntly. "I'd rather put up with a two-hour lecture from my old landlady than go through all that again. Goodnight, Alastair."

"Mmmm," Alastair murmured. "This needs thinking about."

To save him coming up with any more bright ideas, Arthur put out a few feelers himself in the next few days in his lunch hour and struck lucky. Calling in at the local newspaper office on the off chance he asked if they had a need for any fillers. "As a matter of fact," reflected the first editor he sought out, called Reg, who turned out to be an old school chum, "there seems to be a sudden rise in 'down and outs' these days – you know, street musicians and so forth. Might be worth looking into – perhaps a short piece, say a couple of interviews, that sort of thing. Any interest?"

Arthur coughed to disguise a guilty start. "No problem, I'll get onto it right away," and tottered off, turning over in his mind the best way of going about it.

When Alastair heard the news, he gave a whoop of joy and rubbed his hands.

"You are looking at your first candidate for an interview – seek no further. Now let me see, put me down as a poor old man who has been out of work with ten children and a wife ill from worrying about..." he searched his mind.

"About all the lies you've been telling," Arthur added helpfully.

"A little more shoulder-to-shoulder stuff, if you don't mind, laddie." He regarded his friend reproachfully and lay back on the couch, looking dreamily into the distance. "How about making it a round dozen little perishers, all yelling their heads off – that would make it sound a bit more heart-rending."

"Leave it to me," Arthur cut him off shortly. "I'll think of something."

"Do so, laddie, but you're missing out on some fantastic soul-searching stuff when I set my mind to it. You're missing a real treat."

Despite the offer of help, Arthur knocked out a suitable piece and delivered it on the way to work. It must have struck a chord because the editor was onto him the next day and commissioned a follow-up series, as he put it 'on the lack of job opportunities facing the young people today.' Not only that, but he presented Arthur with a very welcome advance that sent Alastair into raptures.

"Fair's fair." He eyed the money hungrily. "What about all the help I gave you for the background material? It's not that I begrudge your good fortune, laddie, but cough up. Otherwise, my dear old landlady will be throwing us out into the street."

"Oh, all right," Arthur agreed, handing over a note. "That'll help towards the rent then."

"Is that all you can spare?" he grumbled, "after all the work I put into it." He added craftily, "And there was I going to find you all that extra help I promised to make your workload easier back at the office?"

Heaving a sigh, Arthur peeled off another one. "There, that's all I can afford. I've got to pay off my fine as well, remember? That's a bit extra for the rent."

Alastair kissed each note. "Bless you, mate." He tucked the notes away and after some thought reached for his jacket.

"Blow that for lark – I'm off to celebrate," he declared with sudden enthusiasm. "This'll pay for my night out as well." He escaped before his friend could think of anything cutting enough to adequately express his feelings on the subject.

The next morning, Arthur told Nancy about Alastair's promises, tactfully leaving out details of their escapade with the banjo. She seemed delighted with the news, but after taking a closer look at him, she remarked candidly, "Well, I can't say you seem overjoyed at the news."

Arthur hesitated, not wishing to overburden her with his personal problems, but after a few discreet nudges he found himself telling her all about his bust-up with Jenny and how desperate he felt about the situation.

"You poor thing," she sympathised after hearing about it. "I've been through that kind of thing myself at one time or another. I tell you what," she said with a determined toss of her head, "leave it to me, I'll see what I can do. I'm seeing Jenny tonight. I can't promise anything, mind you. Meanwhile, if you feel confident enough, I'll open up that other machine and see how we get on. Come on, chin up."

Arthur forced a smile and crossed his fingers, hoping for a miracle to happen.

Well, it did happen, but not in the way he expected.

He didn't see anything of his friend that evening and when Alastair eventually returned, he lay on the bed, blissfully content. "I told you that everything would come out all right, Arthur. Just you wait and see."

Waltzing in to the office the next morning, Alastair struck a dramatic pose and flung out his arms. "There you are, how about that. May I present your new assistant – Miss Doris Leeds."

After a pregnant pause, the door burst open again and Jenny appeared, oblivious to the drama unfolding in front of her.

"Oh, Arthur, if only I'd have known – what you must think of me. Nancy's told me all about it," she began and was about to fling herself forward full of remorse when she stopped short at the sight of Doris and swayed. "No, I don't believe it, not again," she protested with a wail and turned on her heel.

"Wait – Jenny, I can explain," Arthur begged. But the next moment she had gone.

"Oh no," gasped Nancy. "That's torn it."

9

SOMETHING FISHY

While Arthur was trying to get over the traumatic shock of losing Jenny yet again, the new recruit piped up as if nothing had happened. "Hello," she introduced herself lightly. "Haven't we met before?"

He snorted bitterly. "You can say that again. You're the one who ruined my chances with Jenny by trashing my bedroom and making her think the worst."

Before answering, Doris began to apply some lipstick using what looked like the very mirror that Alastair had lost. Unconcerned, she pouted at him virtuously, carrying on with her artwork. "I always say a little bit of rain doesn't do anyone any harm. Anyway, she had it coming to her. Perhaps it will teach her a lesson not to pinch my boyfriends."

"You had more than one, did you?" he remarked cuttingly.

"Not anymore." She put her lipstick away regretfully. "Anyway, I say better luck next time. I must say, that friend of yours does look rather nice," she added dreamily, fixing her sights on Alastair at the counter. "I hear he's going to be promoted to chief cashier shortly."

"If you believe that, you'll believe anything," he replied, cutting her off coldly and turning away to catch up on his work.

Unabashed, she went on, "Looks as if I'm not the only one," nodding at two new arrivals who had just come in.

Annoyed at her continued interruption, he glanced up to see the manager leading a young man in their direction, both involved in a private discussion.

"Ah, there we are," said the manager, breaking off. "I see in addition to acquiring Miss Leeds, for which I must thank young Stringer, I am delighted to say that we now have another recruit to add to our team – Mr Brown."

He bestowed another of his expansive beams. "I think that completes the picture. I'll leave him in your good hands, Miss Slimsby. Oh, and by the way, if things start looking up as I said they would you'll all be in line for a bonus at this rate."

"Thank you, sir." Nancy took over, introducing herself and adding, "I have been allocated the job of teaching you all how to use these machines – may I ask if either of you has had any previous experience of this nature?"

"I did a course as a secretary before joining Whites Hotel," Doris Leeds offered quickly, to establish her bona fides.

"And what about you, Mr Brown?"

"I've done just about everything – shoe boy, waiter, salesman – you name it," replied Mr Brown engagingly. "You can call me Turk, everyone else does."

"Right," acknowledged Nancy, lifting an eyebrow at Arthur, unimpressed by the wealth of information. "Let's get down to it."

So began the birth of the bank's so-called team of electronic operators. Despite all the odds stacked against it, the system seemed to work, in fits and starts, and gained strength as they went along. Which was just as well, because before long the old customers started coming back and the extra pressure on the cashiers built up to such an extent that soon the pace began to tell.

Alastair was the first one to cotton on to the reason. "You know why, old lad. The manager's gone and put their deposit interest up to encourage them, no wonder they're flocking in."

He wiped his forehead after a hectic session at the counter and groaned, "So much for that bonus MacDougal was talking about and hasn't happened. Who said becoming a blasted cashier was the first step to promotion? I wished I'd never volunteered. I should have opted for foreign exchange like old Jenkins – he has damn all to do all day. Failing that, maybe I should have gone for your job, Arthur, bashing away at that wretched keyboard of yours."

Arthur ignored the jibe. "Helps to keep my mind off other things," he answered shortly, trying to avert his gaze from the girl next to him who reminded him so much of his lost love.

"You should have told me." Alastair caught the reproof in his voice and added hastily, "So you did. Well," he braced himself, "here we go," he quoted, "into the valley of death rode the six hundred, or something damn silly like that."

As the days went by, Arthur did his best to concentrate on his work to help him keep his mind from dwelling on Jenny and what might have been. If it wasn't for the sisterly understanding of Nancy, he was sure he would have cracked up in the process.

"Don't worry, Arthur," she kept consoling him, "as soon as I find out what's happened to Jenny, I'll let you know. I think someone was saying she was hoping to go on some course or other." It was all he had to go on, but it was enough to leave him some glimmer of a better time to come for her, little as it was.

Meanwhile, all was not well at the counter as soon as the queues began to build up. The first to crack under the strain was the first cashier, Mr Symmonds. After mislaying a bag of small change and getting in a muddle about where everything was, he finally gave up, objecting in no uncertain terms about the heavy load of extra work he had to deal with.

Seizing the opportunity, the manager called him into his office and told him bluntly he was not fit enough to carry on. Arthur felt that, in a way, Symmonds was glad the decision was taken for him. Before leaving, he shook Arthur by the hand as he said a sad goodbye and told him not to worry. "We can only do our best." He regarded Arthur in a fatherly way. "Anyway, you'll be off to do your national service next year, so you don't have to worry about banking for a while." He added confidentially, "And I don't think my old friend Mr Jenkins will stand it much longer, either."

He was quite right. Within a week, the chief clerk threw in the towel after hot words were exchanged over the sheer size of the work accumulating, and coming on top of his trenchant views about the reorganisation, it was enough to speed his departure.

The manager lost no time in making new arrangements. In a few days, he was introducing a new cashier, James Rook by name, or as Alastair was quick to find a new name for him – Jimmy 'the crook.' "He's hopeless, old lad – I swear he doesn't know anything about banking. He can't even add up his till at the end of the day. Where did the old man dig him up?"

Glancing around, Arthur warned him cautiously, "I should watch what you're saying. You never know who's listening."

"Who cares?" He sounded unexpectedly defiant, unlike his normal brash self. "You mark my words, he won't be satisfied until he's got rid of the lot of us the way he's going. After this, nothing else could possibly be worse."

Meanwhile, at the Head Office of Automatic Machines Ltd., Jenny was wrestling with her own demons of uncertainty and seething with fury at the thought of what her half-sister, Doris, was doing at that moment, established in the same bank where Arthur was working. She could imagine her, actually sitting cheek by jowl, as the saying goes, and able to take advantage of the situation, as she knew she would, at every opportunity. "Ugh," she registered her disgust to herself.

Taking note of every toss of her head and the furious mutterings that were going on every now and then when she thought she was unobserved, her manager, George, became increasingly concerned at her behaviour. Taking advantage of their easy-going relationship, he enquired half-jokingly, "Not still worried about that installation at the bank, are you? I thought that was all sorted."

Coming out of her daydream, Jenny apologised. "I'm sorry, I don't know what you must think of me – it's nothing to do with that."

"Than what is it, if I may ask? You don't look your normal sunny self, if I may say so."

As she hesitated, anguished at the opportunity she had blown after seeing her sister sitting next to Arthur and not plucking up the courage to speak to him, she found George settling down next to her, prepared to listen and offer advice if it were needed, knowing that business was slacking off at that hour of the day.

"It's all rather personal," she began, and seeing the encouraging look of understanding he gave, some of her hopes and fears began to pour out.

"Wow," he commented. "That's certainly a humdinger of a situation you've got there. Hm, what was this character, 'Stringer' did you say," she nodded wanly, "think he was up to, the idiot, bringing that lass of yours into the office, knowing how things stood between you? D'you think it was deliberate?"

"No," she admitted, trying to be fair. "He probably thought he was being helpful, in his own nutty way." She grimaced. "I hear from Nancy that he seems quite keen on her."

"Sounds as if that's your answer." He jumped at the answer triumphantly. "Well, if it's your sister – or half-sister I should have said – involved, you should be able to handle it. It's all in the family, after all. It's not as if you can't talk to her. So, what are you going to do about it?"

Jenny looked miserable. "You don't understand," she said and filled him in on the background to the family feud, ending, "I just don't know what to do."

He leaned forward, eager to offer his own solution. "I know what I would do if I were you."

"What's that?" she asked cautiously."

"Why, I'd go and make myself known to this Stringer character and flirt with him if necessary. That would make your Arthur sit up and take notice. Might stir him up – a bit of competition wouldn't do any harm."

"Do you really think so?" Jenny said dubiously. "It might put him off me altogether."

"Nonsense, if he's the sort of man I'm sure he is, it will give him something to think about. In any case," he became serious, "from what you are saying, I don't like the way things are shaping up in that bank of yours. Sounds like a murky situation all round to me. Don't forget, our company's account is at that branch, making us one of their largest clients, so we would only be protecting our interests to know what's going on there – you can take that as official."

"So, you want me to do some digging, you mean," she said wonderingly, "acting as some sort of a snoop."

"Let's say, you'd be acting as our official investigator." He amended the phrase, making it sound official.

"D'you know, I think I will," she decided making up her mind, fired by his suggestion.

Next day after lunch, armed with her official status, she

appeared unexpectedly at the bank counter asking to see Alastair in a raised tone, hoping that her voice could be heard by the rest of the staff, notably by both Arthur and Doris.

Her request woke up Harris, the second cashier, who apologised, informing her that Alastair was stepping aside for a break, and immediately went off to fetch him. As Alastair appeared looking slightly apprehensive, she put out her hand to greet him warmly, hoping she would sound convincing.

"So nice to meet you, Mr Stringer, I've heard so much about you, or should I call you Alastair?"

"By all means, Miss Young." He fingered his collar, glancing apologetically at Arthur and Doris as he did so.

"I am most anxious to make sure our equipment is perfectly safe after all the trouble you've been having lately."

"Er, perhaps it would be better if we had a word in the visitor's reception," he answered nervously, casting a swift look around, fearful at being overheard. "If you will come around inside, allow me."

Arthur almost leapt out of his seat at the sound of her familiar voice, and so, he could see, did Doris. He waited breathlessly to hear further, but his hopes were dashed as she swept past, her eyes averted, accompanied by Alastair who escorted her to an inner cubicle, explaining hastily in passing, "Just bringing her up to date on the equipment and things."

Inside, she got down to business with a broadside after his assurances that everything was going splendidly and put the question she had asked Arthur in all innocence when they first met. "What my manager cannot understand, Alastair, is how the thieves knew that the manager would be safely out of his office when the break-in occurred?"

Fingering his collar again, Alastair hunted around for a suitably acceptable excuse. "Yes, I'm glad you asked me that. We thought that was a bit odd ourselves, but I suppose when this sort of thing happens, they have to spend time planning it all in advance." After warming up to his theme, he launched into a garbled account of what might have occurred, based entirely on his fertile imagination.

Interrupting him and delving into her handbag, Jenny produced a folded document. "Let me see, according to the statement made by the police who were there shortly afterwards, it appears that you were actually present when the robbery took place, seemingly only minutes after the stolen trolley collided with a passing van. Is this true? I'm sure you will be able to explain that?" She smiled engagingly.

He produced a handkerchief and mopped his brow. "Yes, quite. I wonder if we could talk this over more informally, in a dinner perhaps where we are not, shall I say, um, restricted by an office environment, where we can speak more freely. What shall we say, Friday perhaps?"

"Well, that's very kind of you, if it's not conflicting with any other engagement you might have. I must check on the date and let you know."

"Not at all, Jenny, if I may call you that. I'm sure we could clear this up so much more easily in the right atmosphere. Shall we say eight o'clock, how would that suit you?"

Appearing gratified by the offer, Jenny said, "Where do you suggest – they say the Whites Hotel is quite well thought of."

"Not there," interrupted Alastair hastily, "I hear the place has gone right down recently. No, what about the Swan round the corner. That would be more..." he searched for an apt description.

"More suitable?"

"Exactly," agreed Alastair, relieved at the choice. "Just let me know when you're free, and we'll fix a date. And now if you'll excuse me, we are rather short of cashiers at the moment."

"Of course," demurred Jenny, allowing herself to be shown out, casting a proprietary glance at the others as she did so.

"What's this I hear – a cosy tete-a-tete at the Swan?" demanded Nancy slyly, overhearing.

Casting a wild look around, Alastair flung up his hands. "Well, I've got to be polite to the customers, haven't I. Stands to reason." Feeling his appeal was wasted, he whispered to Arthur in anguish, "Got to lush her up, old lad, she's asking too many blasted questions."

"What about me?" piped up Doris, offended at the news. "Aren't I good enough?"

"Of course you are, my precious," placated Alastair hurriedly. "What about tomorrow night – same time, at the Whites."

"I thought you told her that the Whites Hotel was not good enough," accused Doris, not letting him off the hook.

"That was for an entirely different reason," he bluffed, aware that he was losing ground.

"Tell you what, why don't we make it a regular date, just the two of us – what do you say?"

"All right, if you mean it." She appeared mollified.

As if in a trance, Alastair passed a weary hand over his face. "I think I need a drink, old boy, what about it?"

"It's only three o'clock." Arthur squashed his hopes. "You'll have to cash up first."

At the mention of cash, Alastair winced and lowered his voice. "How the devil am I going to afford taking them both out, and now I've promised her a regular treat... I ask you."

"You could always find time to rob a bank," joked Arthur.

"Do you mind, old lad? This is no laughing matter."

"There's always the banjo to fall back on," suggested Arthur helpfully.

Alastair quivered. "Don't even mention the word." He racked his brain. "There must be some other way of making some extra cash. What about those articles of yours – any chance of rustling up any more money earners where that came from? I could always mug up some more family details – you know, all that stuff about a wife and ten starving children and anything else I can think of."

"If you can think up any useful ideas," Arthur replied cautiously, "I don't mind trying – not all that rubbish you were coming up with last time."

"I'll think of something," Alastair promised, rubbing his arm affectionately. "You know you can rely on your old mate. I'm full of ideas. What about a piece on the tourist trade – it's about that time of the year when they all come piling in and spending dollars. We could get Whites Hotel involved; they'd jump at the chance. No, on second thoughts," he dismissed the thought reluctantly, "that would mean hiring out an army of waiters."

"What about how you saved the day stopping that bank robbery," Arthur asked sarcastically.

He groaned. "Don't remind me, old lad. I've got to think up some quick answers for that Jenny of yours when I take her out. And where am I to get the funds for that? I tell you, I'm ruined before I start."

Even as he spoke, a familiar face from the past appeared at the counter calling for service, as if to contradict his statement. Seeing him, Alastair clutched Arthur's arm feverishly. "Don't look now, Arthur," he swallowed, "but do you see who I see?"

Following his gaze, Arthur closed his eyes in disbelief. For the customer standing there was none other than the learned magistrate who they last saw on that fateful day when he passed sentence, leaving them to fork out twenty-seven pounds without an option.

"He's signalling to me," panicked Alastair.

"You'd better go and see," his friend urged. "There's no one else on the counter."

Like a man in a trance, Alastair obeyed the summons reluctantly and after a short consultation, holding a sheet of paper in front of his face in a desperate bid to hide his identity, escorted the magistrate into the manager's inner sanctum.

Fifteen minutes later, he emerged, looking shaken. "He kept on calling me Tom Brown," he uttered brokenly.

"Well, that's the only name he knows you by," Arthur agreed. "What did our manager say to that?"

"What didn't he say." He ran a hand through his hair in despair. "There goes my bonus."

"Did old MacDougal let on what our real names were?"

"No." He thought back. "That's the funny part about it – he just told me afterwards to watch my step." Then Alastair harked back to his earlier grievance. "What the devil am I going to do now – I've already spent half of what I put by, what with all these extra expenses, like free meals." Thinking back, his voice took on a rebellious tone. "Wait a minute; there's something fishy about that man. Why did he keep quiet about my name? I don't know what the reason was, but I intend to find out."

"Well, the best of luck," Arthur said, imagining that his friend was indulging in his usual bout of wishful thinking. "You'd better get back before the queue builds up again."

"I mean it this time," his friend said doggedly, "you'll see."

It wasn't until he got back to their digs that he encountered Alastair again and this time he was looking strangely satisfied with himself. "I knew it, I knew he was up to no good," he burst out. "I hung around outside his office and overheard him jawing about it with that new cashier of ours. They sounded as thick as thieves."

"I hope they didn't see you." Arthur felt concerned. Although he viewed some of his friend's actions as a trifle outrageous at times, he didn't want him to jeopardise his position now he was a cashier and said so.

"No chance of that now," Alastair said with growing

certainty. "Now he knows I'm onto him; he'll have to watch his step."

Arthur shook his head dubiously. "I'm not so sure; he's a tough customer, our manager. You never know what he might do."

However, whatever suspicions Alastair may have harboured appeared to have vanished overnight, because next morning, after being called unexpectedly into the manager's office, he came out grinning all over his face and went out of his way to allay any fears anyone might have had.

"Suspicions, lord no, whatever gave you that idea," he declared serenely. "Rory and me are like ham and eggs."

"Rory?" Arthur queried incredulously. "How long has this been going on?"

"Never you mind," Alastair countered mysteriously and added gleefully, "And you'll never guess – I've got my bonus back, so I don't have to worry about those extra expenses.

I can afford to take Jenny out after all."

As Arthur pondered over this miraculous change of heart, he noticed that Doris was basking in the attention paid to her by the new recruit, Turk Brown, as he called himself.

Being stuck on the counter, Alastair missed all the amorous gambits, but as soon as he could tear himself away from the counter, he found himself in the unaccustomed position of fighting off a rival. "It's not on, old man," he complained to Arthur later, as soon as they got back to his digs. "Who is this upstart – another crony of our manager?"

Noting that he had consigned the manager to a less flattering rating, Arthur remarked sarcastically, "So the ham and eggs have reached their 'sell by' date? Sounds as if she's got both of you on the run." He found he had no sympathy for his friend after the harm Doris had caused Jenny.

"Do me a favour, old lad; I haven't got eyes in the back of my neck. Why can't you have a word with her? She's sitting right next to you after all. Pitch it as strong as you can." He massaged Arthur's shoulder tenderly. "Don't forget we're old mates, aren't we?"

"It's all your fault," Arthur reminded him. "You shouldn't have brought her here in the first place – it ruined any chance I had of making it up with Jenny."

"But I did it all for you," he pointed out with an injured air. "That's all the thanks I get."

∾

Keen to find out how Jenny got on with Alastair after adopting his advice, George tackled her next morning.

"Well, how is our femme fatale getting on with her mission?" he enquired eagerly. "Did it work?"

"Yes," she answered thoughtfully, "in more ways than one. I think what I've discovered raises more questions than it provides answers."

"Tell me more," he invited, settling back and pushing his files to one side. "This sounds more like it."

Jenny marshalled her thoughts. "I was expecting to find him full of jitters after me asking all those awkward questions about that robbery of theirs, but he brushed them off as mere gossip."

"I thought the manager had explained about that. I gather they had a request, apparently from head office, about an emergency delivery for the Red Cross."

"So he said," she went on, glossing over the details in case it might implicate Arthur in some way. "He gave me a lot of hogwash about that, and the manager thinks he saved the day after they recovered all the money. But listen to this, I learnt something that's far more interesting."

"I'm all agog."

"What, oh, I see. Well, apparently, according to Nancy, the cashiers were getting so overworked with all the new customers they were getting after he bumped up their deposit rates that they cracked up under the strain and the chief clerk and the first cashier were given the boot."

"Go on." George was getting worked up. "What happened next?"

"They brought in some weird new character as first cashier, called James Rook – who Alastair nicknamed 'Jimmy the Crook' and, wait for it – he claims that Rook knows nothing about banking at all, he can't even balance his till. What do you think about that?"

George whistled. "Is there more?"

"You bet there is." Her eyes glowed. "That clown Alastair and his friend got hauled up before the beak about some trifling offence," she skated over the details, "and the next thing this magistrate turns up at the branch and finds Alastair had passed himself off with an alias and the manager didn't even give away their real names."

George tut-tutted. "Guarding the bank's reputation, no doubt."

"But it was enough to arouse Alastair's suspicions apparently, and he swore he would investigate after claiming the manager and this new cashier of his were heard in cahoots thick as thieves – and because of his snooping he lost his bonus the manager promised them."

"That does sound odd."

"Not only that. Next morning Alastair turned up saying everything was fine and that he and Rory, as he called the manager, were like ham and eggs."

"'Ham and eggs'? How extraordinary. And what about his bonus?"

"No problem, he said he's had it restored. Can you explain that, because I can't."

"It all sounds extremely fishy to me. I think you've done an outstanding job there, Jenny. I wouldn't be surprised if it doesn't earn you some well-deserved promotion." He gathered his papers together, meditating. "After hearing all that, I expect they'll be wondering whether it's safe to leave their account at that branch much longer. That manager of theirs sounds a bit of a rascal to me, totally unfit to be a manager, I would have thought. And he used to be in the SAS as well, who'd have thought it. And as for that Alastair, I shouldn't think he's very popular either, cosying up to the manager like that." He shook his head disapprovingly. "What is the world coming to?"

10

WAITING FOR THE RIGHT MOMENT

After witnessing Jenny cutting him dead and her sudden friendship with Alastair, Arthur became extremely despondent, and despite the efforts of Nancy to cheer him up, he felt let down by his friend and was beginning to feel he no longer wanted to have anything to do with him. He was so upset by it all that he was in two minds to look for another job – anywhere that didn't constantly remind him of the love he had lost. In fact, he was in such a depressed state of mind he felt at times like jumping off the nearest bridge and ending it all.

Whatever the future held for him, he couldn't stand listening to Alastair and about his love life any longer. He was already regretting his decision to share the digs and wondered how to put it in words that would not offend his friend. What he needed was as an excuse he could use to enable him to return to his old lodgings, despite the thought of having to deal with Mrs Musgrove again. Finally, it was the state of his clothes that provided an answer. Thinking of all his things he left behind, he hit upon it as the ideal solution.

"Alastair, I'm badly in need of a fresh outfit – this lot I'm wearing will have to go to the laundry," he announced, breaking the news as gently as possible, thinking his friend might be upset at losing a share of the rent.

To his surprise, Alastair seemed taken with the idea and became quite keen at the thought. "That's all right, old man. It'll leave me free to invite Doris – I mean my other friends – around for an evening. What a splendid idea. I'll need to freshen the place up a bit first, of course," he added cheekily, warding his friend off with a laugh as he made to throw a cushion at him.

Arthur had to admit that as he finally arrived back at his old digs after so long, he was feeling a little nervous at the reception he might get. Instead of the expected lengthy reproaches, however, to his surprise, he was met by Mrs Musgrove herself who took him to one side and mysteriously put a finger to her lips, whispering, "Shush."

Fearing that someone had recently suffered a near-fatal accident and that the Colonel might have decided that his pig-sticking days were over, he followed her example and tiptoed into the television room, fearing the worst. As soon as he got inside, he was warmly greeted by his landlady. "How lovely to see you again, Mr Conway. Is your friend with you?"

"No, I'm afraid not," he began, but she shushed him again. "It's Ben, that dog of hers – he's up to his naughty tricks as usual," she gushed. "I was afraid we might wake him up again." From her expression, he concluded that the experience was still fresh in her mind.

Arthur was bewildered. "I thought Jenny, I mean, Miss Young had taken Ben away with her."

"She had, but the wee lass had to go on a course, and she asked if I could look after him while she was away." By the satisfied way she put it, he assumed that the arrangement had been particularly beneficial to her bank balance.

"How long is she going to be away?" he asked anxiously, keen to find out how he could get in touch with her.

"Goodness me, I thought you might be the first to know." She laughed girlishly, much to his embarrassment. "Never mind, now you are here, all our little problems will be over. I know, you don't have to tell me – you can't wait to look after him again until Miss Young returns. How wonderful." She drew in a deep breath of satisfaction.

"Me? Look after him! But I have my job to see to." He panicked.

"Yes, but when you get home," she cooed, "darling Ben will be waiting to greet you."

"How... um, jolly," he agreed wanly. As he turned to go upstairs and nerve himself to the task, he asked, "Where are all the other lodgers, by the way," thinking it all seemed rather quiet.

"They decided to go for a walk," she said quickly, smiling nervously. "It's such a lovely evening. They couldn't wait to make the most of it."

Arthur tried to imagine all the other tenants setting off on a group outing together and failed to visualise the glowing picture she painted.

"They were so disappointed you'd be doing them out of their favourite pastime of taking yon Ben out for a walk," she cooed, dismissing from her mind the jubilant noises her lodgers made when they were told about his return.

"Overjoyed, were they?" Arthur marvelled at the picture she painted.

"Oh, yes. They were absolutely heartbroken when I told them. One of them sobbed on my shoulder he was so upset, the poor man."

Listening to her glowing account, Arthur wondered for a moment whether she was talking about the same lodgers he remembered from his previous visit.

"Oh yes," Mrs Musgrove went on dreamily, drawing on her own world of fantasy. "You ought to try it yourself, Arthur," she added persuasively. "Such a lovely, obedient animal is Ben; he can't wait to go out for his walkies. It will do you all the good in the world. There's nothing he likes better than a stroll in the evening, it makes a beautiful end of his day, especially when he has his loving friends around him. You should hear what they say about that lovely gorgeous dog. They love him so much."

Arthur tried his best to imagine such a transformation and failed. "Right, well I'll turn in for a bit of shut-eye. Goodnight, Mrs Musgrove."

"Goodnight, Arthur." She beamed. "I do hope you get a good night's rest." She added roguishly, "I know someone who can't wait to see you again."

She was quite right. As soon as Ben heard him coming up the stairs, he could hear the dog starting to hurl himself at the door. When he opened it, he staggered back with the dog frantically licking his face. Before Ben could do any more damage, Arthur remembered it was time for him to do his wees and hauled him down to the back door. After it was all over, the dog renewed his welcome as if he hadn't seen him in a month of Sundays. By the time he managed to get him watered and fed, it was well past midnight. It was then he vowed to himself that if ever Jenny and he managed to get back together again, there would have to be a new set of rules regarding Ben's behaviour. Otherwise their days would be ruined, not to mention the nights.

By the next morning, it was a very battered and weary Arthur Conway who made his way to the office. In fact, the only way he could leave the room was to put down a tempting dish of food to attract the dog's attention while he slipped out unobserved.

He even managed to enter the office without being seen by Stuart and having to undergo his sartorial inspection, which he considered to be a major achievement. However, he was soon waylaid by Alastair who seemed to be more concerned with his current affair, complaining bitterly that they would have to do something about that pest, Turk, who now spent most of his allotted hours pestering Doris who appeared to be preening herself at the amount of attention she was receiving.

"How can I concentrate on my work, when that blighter is pestering Doris behind my back, I ask you," he demanded, putting on an injured expression. "Can't you do something, old lad? You're sitting right next to her, after all."

Thinking his attitude was a bit thick after his blatant efforts to take Jenny out, Arthur cut him short. "I thought your attention was being directed elsewhere. Make up your mind, which one are you after."

Alastair adopted an injured air. "Just because I had a chat with your Jenny to steer her off that little trouble we had, I'm accused of being her admirer – I call that a bit thick. I'm surprised at you, old lad. I thought we were old buddies." His voice took on a trembling appeal of old. "Don't let me down at this stage, old friend. I rely on you to keep an eye on that Turk character and make sure he doesn't mess up my chances with Doris."

"It wasn't me who had that little trouble, "Arthur reminded him. "You were the one who got me into it in the first place. If old Morrissey hadn't turned up when he did, you'd have been in real trouble. You wouldn't have had the time to worry about girlfriends."

"Your words wound me, old fruit. They positively cut me to the quick – do your best, otherwise me chances are ruined, absolutely ruined."

Cutting his friend short, Arthur managed to tear himself free and was able to bring Nancy up to date about Jenny's movements. But what she told him in return was enough to make him wonder whether he would ever see Jenny again. "You'll never guess," Nancy informed him proudly, "our Jenny is expected to be promoted to manager when she's finished that course you were telling me about."

"Great." Arthur managed to convey his congratulations before asking mournfully, "Does that mean we'll never see her again?"

Nancy pursed her lips. "Well, she has to give us clearance at some point now the equipment is fully working, but once that's finished, I suppose she'll be moving around quite a lot to look after some of the company's other installations."

Arthur mulled over the implications. Whilst pleased at Jenny's prospects, he viewed the change with a heavy heart, knowing how little he had to offer her, and began to doubt whether they would ever come together again.

His musings were interrupted by the appearance of the manager who beckoned him over.

"Sir?"

"Ah, Conway, will you arrange for someone to bring some sandwiches into my office in ten minutes or so – I'm expecting some important visitors. My new secretary hasn't turned up yet."

"Yes, of course, sir," he said immediately, wondering who they might be.

"I've ordered the sandwiches. You'll find them down in the basement with the rest of the tea things – get Harris, the second cashier, to show you – he knows where everything is." With that parting instruction, he turned and disappeared from view.

Searching for Harris, Arthur found him dozing at the counter, taking advantage of one of the lulls between serving customers, and acquainted him with news of the arrivals.

"Of course, you don't know where to find anything," he said, uncoiling himself half-heartedly. "I'd better come down and show you – I can't spend too much time at it mind you, we're a bit busy at the moment."

Following him down the stairs, they both had to duck as they went.

"You'll have to be careful," Harris warned. "Mind the steps; it's a little primitive down here. We should have done something about it years ago. The old man was too busy playing with his trains to think about having it done."

He watched Harris assembling the cups, plates and sandwiches on a tray when there was a shout from above. "Sorry, I must dash," he excused himself apologetically. "Sounds as if they need me on top."

"Wait a minute, how am I going to get that lot upstairs?" Arthur asked desperately, taking in the size of the loaded tray.

"Oh, I forgot to mention, there's a lift in the cupboard over there. You just load the tray in and pull the rope to haul it up – sorry, I must go." With that parting advice, he left hurriedly.

Gingerly lifting the tray and carefully placing it into the lift as instructed, Arthur tried to start it off on its upward journey by giving the rope inside the opening a gentle tug, but nothing happened. The tray remained where it was. He gave it another more forceful yank with the same result. Peering inside, he noticed that the rope seemed to have become tangled up somewhere inside above his head, but try as he might, he was unable to grab hold of anything, and it remained out of reach. Not to be outdone, he climbed on a chair and reached up inside to get a better grip.

Before he knew what was happening, he lost his balance and ended up sitting beside the tray and almost immediately the tray and its contents started moving up inside the lift shaft, and the kitchen sank slowly out of sight. Before he could do anything, the lift gave a sudden lurch and came to a halt, ending up under a desk in the very room where the visitors were sitting.

Scarcely afraid to breathe in case he gave his presence away, he listened to what they were saying, hoping he would be able to pick up some clue that would help to explain Alastair's recent odd relationship with the manager.

The next minute he heard a voice and the familiarity of the tones electrified him. It was Rook, the one Alastair had nicknamed Jim the Crook – no wonder Harris was finding it difficult to cope on the counter without the first cashier. The very first words he uttered made it abundantly clear that he had no previous experience of banking.

"For Pete's sake, Rory, when are we going to bust this joint – what are we waiting for?"

"Don't rush me." Arthur caught a glimpse of his feet passing the cubby hole in front of him and shrank back.

"We've got to wait for the right moment," he heard the manager insist, "when I know those nuts out there have filled the strong room to bursting point. That's when I press the button and not before. Why d'you think I went to all the trouble to bring in that new equipment and jack up the interest rates – to draw the crowd in, that's why. Now they can't wait to join the queue – the suckers."

"Gee, that's all very well, but I don't like it," he heard Rook complain. "That nosy parker Stringer is suspicious – he keeps asking me all sorts of awkward questions. D'you know what? I even heard him tell that guy Conway I don't know anything about banking, I ask you."

"Well, you don't. Anyone can see that."

"How can you say that, boss?" he said aggrieved. "I've busted more banks than he's had hot dinners."

MacDougal sighed with exasperation. "He's not talking about that kind of banking, dumbhead. He means dealing with those mutts out there – the paying customers."

"Oh, that's different – I thought he was talking about me getting in there amongst the tumblers. You know me, boss, nobody can touch me in dat department – ask anyone in the business."

"How many times do I have to tell you – we don't need to open the vault that way, we've got the keys."

"Okay, but I don't like the way things are stacking up. That guy gives me the willies – he'll be spouting off about me up at that head office of yours at this rate. I feel it in me bones. What do we do if that happens – he'll sing like a canary."

"No chance." MacDougal was quite definite on that point.

"How can you be so sure, boss?"

"Because... if you must know, I've squared him, that's what."

"Yeah, what with?"

Losing his patience, McDougal snapped, "I'm telling you, he came in asking all sorts of damn fool questions in that superior tone of his the other day until I couldn't stand it any longer, like you said and," he admitted at last, "if you want to know, I promised him a cut if he kept quiet."

"But boss," the other said sounding injured, "why didn't you tell me? I could've taken him down a dark alley and settled his hash, and nobody would have been any the wiser. It would have saved you all that trouble, believe me."

"That's all we want, you dumb cluck. Are you trying to ruin everything at this stage? That's the last thing we need. Talk sense. Don't worry. I've got that guy in such a state worrying about his love life, he hasn't got time to think of anything else. The only cut he'll get is in the neck at this rate. Who's that?" He broke off impatiently.

There was a knock on the door and the familiar tones of the bank's recent recruit butted in, the last person Arthur was expecting. "Hi, it's me. Let me in; I've got something to tell you."

"Oh, Turk, it's you. Come in – what is it?" said MacDougal relieved at the interruption.

Turk eased himself in and glanced around furtively. "It's okay to talk?" Assured on that point, he loosened up. "Listen,

I've been chatting that Doris bird up, like you said, to keep that menace Stringer occupied so's he doesn't keep asking too many questions and guess what?"

"Well, spit it out." Jimmy Rook eyed him darkly, annoyed at losing the focus of attention.

Ignoring him, Turk couldn't wait to break the news. "It looks as if we've got to put the brakes on that plan of yours, boss. I've just heard something that could put a jemmy in the works."

"What's that?" demanded MacDougal and Jimmy simultaneously.

"You know that bird Jenny, who was around the other week? Well, that friend of hers, Nancy, has told Conway she needs to come and sign off the new equipment sometime soon, so it looks as if we'll have to call everything off until she's gone. We don't want her around poking her nose in just at the wrong moment – she could put a spanner in the works, and we would be up the creek, no kidding."

"When's she coming?" MacDougal asked urgently.

"She didn't say. Apparently, this Jenny character is on a management course at the moment, and when she's finished, it's on the cards she'll get promoted to manager. Once that happens, the first thing she'll do is to come and inspect the equipment to see if it's working okay."

"Jeez, that's all we need," cursed Jimmy. "Let me take care of her."

"No, you pinhead." MacDougal slapped the table impatiently. "This needs thinking about. We must find out when she's coming, thanks for letting us know, Turk. Meanwhile, keep your nose close to the ground both of you, we can't afford to make any mistakes at this stage. That's all."

"Okay, you're the boss." Jimmy lumbered to his feet. "Better get back before that Harris menace gets the jitters."

Waiting until all sounds of the visitors had gone, Arthur

clambered gingerly out of the lift, catching his head painfully on the desk as he crawled out. As he staggered to his feet, rubbing his neck, he reached out for the handle of the door and, opening it, came face to face with the manager.

11

TORN BETWEEN TWO LOYALTIES

"What the devil are you doing here?"

The tone was so abrupt that Arthur was taken aback. He finally managed to stutter. "Er, the lift got stuck – I was just fixing it."

"Well, see that it doesn't happen again. You were too late, anyway. My guests have gone."

"I'm sorry, sir. I hope your meeting went well?" he said, hoping his remark would quell any suspicions as he edged past.

"Yes, quite well, thank you. See that I'm not disturbed in future." He remained there frowning after Arthur had gone, casting his mind back over what had been said and wondering if it had been too revealing. Undecided for a moment, he finally put a call out for Turk over the tannoy system.

Drumming his fingers on the desk, he told Turk to shut the door when he entered. After he related what had just occurred, he came to a snap decision. "We can't afford to wait for that blasted Jenny woman to come back now – it's mucked up everything. Let's see, today's Thursday... let's make it Saturday."

"Now you're speaking, boss." Turk jerked to life with a joyful spring in his step, glad that all the waiting was over.

"Quiet, you idiot – otherwise the whole place will hear all about it." He reflected. "Yes, Saturday afternoon it is. It'll be quiet out there by then. Most of the dummies will be doing their shopping after lunch, and the vault should be overflowing. Agreed?"

"You betcha," responded Turk hungrily, smacking his lips at the prospect.

"Now, what I want you to do is to take Jimmy somewhere after we've closed and tell him to pencil in a meeting for Friday night seven o'clock sharp to go over the details. I don't want to bring him in here again now. Otherwise, someone might put two and two together – like that young nosey parker Conway who I caught in here after you'd gone."

"Wha-at?" Turk exploded. "Why didn't you tell me that first off – I could have done something about him."

"Now don't you start, I've had a basinful of Jimmy's nutty ideas. If you did anything like that, we'd have the rossers down on us like a ton of bricks."

"Okay, I guess you're the one who gives the orders." Turk got to his feet reassuringly. "I'll make sure he doesn't blow the gaff – and I'll keep an eye on that nosey parker out there – in case he gets up to something."

"You do that, right, that's all. Keep me posted if you hear anything – I'd give a bundle to know what that snake Conway is up to right now."

Aware that he was sitting on a powder keg of vital information, Arthur was in a quandary about what to do for the best. As he sat working, he was feeling increasingly frustrated, knowing that two sets of eyes were fixed on him, watching his every move. He did not dare speak to Nancy, knowing that if he did, her life wouldn't be worth a candle. His only hope was to bide his time and talk it over with Alastair after work.

He wasn't the only one who was worried. His attitude plainly disturbed Nancy, who imagined she must have upset him in some way and was racking her brains to get to the reason behind it. Finding an excuse to stop at his desk, she came out with it, asking him jokingly whether she had offended him in some way.

Embarrassed by her concern and catching a suspicious glance from Turk, he replied in the same vein, pretending he had done something wrong on the machine.

As she leaned over to see, he scribbled on a pad and pushed towards her. It read 'Can't talk now. Urgent – where can I see you after work. Vital.'

Hiding her astonishment, she tapped him playfully on the wrist and said loudly, "Don't be naughty," to give anyone listening the wrong impression and wrote 'usual tearoom.'

Arthur nodded, satisfied, and continued their playacting until Turk looked away rather bored with it all.

To make sure he was not observed after leaving the bank, Arthur spent ten minutes walking around the block to put anyone off before looking up and down the street and diving into the tearoom where they sometimes had their midday break.

"Now, what's it all about?" questioned Nancy in her usual blunt way of approaching a subject. "You looked like a scalded cat out there – you jumped a mile whenever anyone came near you."

Taking a deep breath, Arthur plunged into the story of what he had been through since they last spoke, while Nancy sat there riveted throughout. She sat back at last, stunned. "I can't believe it. Who would imagine that such a thing was possible right in the heart of London – is that what they call 'an inside stand'?"

She took another bewildered look at him after waiting until the waitress left their coffee order. "Who appointed this man MacDougal anyway? Someone must have been round the bend."

Arthur gave a short laugh. "It was our previous manager, Morrissey, who spent his time playing with his toy trains while he was waiting for promotion."

"You must be joking – a manager in charge of a bank playing with trains?"

"That was before Alastair wangled that job up at head office as general manager, of course."

"General manager?" Nancy couldn't believe her ears. "How on earth did he manage to get that?"

"To be fair," Arthur ruminated, "he would have been quite happy left on his own with his trains, but Alastair built up his hopes with some letter of support he got signed, and that's when everything went wrong."

"What happened?"

Arthur was plainly embarrassed. "Well, there was this accident with the trolley full of banknotes, ahem, meant for a special delivery, and things sort of got out of hand. Anyway," he changed the subject before she could ask any more awkward questions, "the ironic result was that he appointed someone to take over who we were told had been a member of the SAS in the war – who he said would be ideal for the job!"

"He certainly was. Sounds a tough one to deal with all right. The question is, what are you going to do about it?"

"Well, from what he said, we've got a bit of breathing space." Arthur reflected. "He's talking about holding off until after Jenny has been in to sign off the equipment... but after catching me in the office after the meeting like that he may be forced to change his plans, we just don't know. Anyway, I thought I'd better tell you to get it off my chest."

"And a good thing you did," emphasised Nancy. "You do realise it's going to put you in real danger if they find out?"

Arthur fiddled with his coffee spoon. "I suppose you could say that."

Seeing him hesitate, Nancy was quite firm. "In that case, don't you think it's time to let the police know and let them decide what's best?"

"I know, I know," agreed Arthur wretchedly, "but I must have a word with Alastair first to see how he's mixed up in it all – if it wasn't for him, I'd never have got the job in the first place."

"I quite understand; it must be very awkward for you."

"You can say that again." Arthur brooded over the situation, torn between two loyalties.

She smiled encouragingly. "Well, let me know if I can be of any help. Meanwhile, I'll have another go at trying to get hold of Jenny. When are you going to see him?"

"As soon as possible is the short answer – directly I get hold of him at his digs, tonight if possible."

When Arthur finally managed to track his friend down, Alastair was humming a gay tune as he entered his rooms. Seeing Arthur waiting for him, he looked more than a little surprised.

"Goodness, what are you doing here? Has your landlady chucked you out already?" Then another thought occurred to him. "How did you get in, by the way? Have you still got your key? Not that it matters, old lad." He gave a nervous laugh. "It's just that I'm expecting a young lady to drop in at any time and it might be a trifle infra dig if you found us, um, if you know what I mean..."

Feeling uncomfortable, as if he was attending a funeral of some close member of the family, Arthur gestured to a chair. "I should sit down if I was you, I've got some news that may come as a bit of a surprise. On second thoughts," he added, "you'd better get yourself a stiff whiskey. Make it a double, and I'll join you."

Alastair did as he was bid and sat down expectantly. "What's happened, has your long-lost aunt pegged out and left you a fortune? If so, you can always rely on me to help you invest it." His voice trailed off at the expression on his friend's face. "Well, out with it. You can trust me, your old friend."

"I'm afraid it's the latter as far as you're concerned," said Arthur bluntly.

After hearing how he had been tricked, Alastair gave a sudden start that wiped the smile off his face and almost left him without a word to say. Recovering with an effort, he waved his hands indignantly.

"Why, the devious skunk... I mean the cheek of the man," he said, covering up his slip. "It's outrageous! Trying to implicate me in his downright dishonest schemes – it's disgusting, unheard of, monstrous. It makes one despair of the human race when you hear such," he searched for the word, "vile, slanderous and diabolical accusations."

"But is it true?"

"True? How can you think such a monumental slur on my character might be true – your old school friend? No, come to think of it, we don't go back that far... well, old buddy, dearest friend," then noticing his protestations didn't seem to have any effect, his voice changed to a tremulous warble. "You don't seriously believe all this..." words failed him.

"But you did seem to change your mind about him rather quickly after you were dead set on exposing him," Arthur reminded him gently.

"Yes, but he assured me I was completely on the wrong track... and I believed him. Did you hear anything like it? Pon my word, if there's any justice in the world someone should be thanking me for getting at the truth. If that's the way people treat you, dammit, I've a good mind to give it all up and emigrate – to some faraway spot in the world, some oasis of peace and serenity where trust is a byword."

"Well if that's the case," suggested Arthur casually, "I suppose the best thing would be to get in touch with that detective we met, what was his name, ah yes, Detective Sergeant Bird, that's the man – he'll know what to do."

Alastair looked alarmed and clutched his arm. "Do no such thing on my account, I implore you, Arthur – he's quite the wrong type to handle such a... delicate matter." He grew quite indignant at the thought and puffed out his cheeks. "Why, he even thought that little trouble with the trolley and the money was all our fault. No, this needs thinking about."

Overlooking the other's willingness to include him in his escapades, Arthur persisted patiently. "So, any bright ideas – we can't just leave it as it is."

"Wait," Alastair garbled. "You heard what they said. They're going to wait until Jenny comes back to sign off that equipment – why, we've got masses of time. You see, it only needs a little calm reasoning to show us what steps to take."

"We'd better come up with something soon – I've already brought Nancy up to date with the situation."

"You've done what? Of all the fatheaded things to do, that takes the biscuit. Are you mad?"

"If I didn't, it might have put her life in danger. She sits right next to the man. It's only fair. You know what Turk's like, no girl's safe with him around."

His friend simmered down. "Perhaps you're right. What's your idea – if you have one," he added grudgingly.

Arthur thought aloud, trying to humour him. "The only concrete evidence is my word against his..."

Alastair came out of a trance. "Yes, yes?"

"All you have to do is to deny you had anything to do with it."

His friend came to life, like the wind freshening up on a boat's sails. "Go on, go on."

"Your best line being that you only did it to keep him quiet while you carried on your investigation."

"By heavens, I believe you've got it, old man." He got up and massaged Arthur's arm affectionately. "I never thought of that – what a splendid wheeze."

"So, we can go ahead as I suggested and report it to the police, so they know what to do?"

Alastair hummed and hawed. "Ah yes, when we've hit on the right time to do it – and make sure you don't tell that Bird character, make it someone else, just to be on the safe side."

"Good, then I'll let Nancy know what we've agreed."

"Yes, I suppose we'd better."

With that concession, Arthur had to be satisfied and left just in time to see Doris letting herself in behind him.

As soon as he got to the office next morning, Nancy drew him aside and whispered discreetly while going through the motions of showing him a statement, "I've heard from Jenny."

Recovering from the good news, Arthur mouthed. "When?"

"She doesn't know – sometime soon."

"Did you tell her?"

"No, I didn't want her worried."

"Good," then louder, "Thank you, Miss Slimsby, I'll take a note of those figures." Making for his desk, he sat down, hoping they were not overheard.

At their tearoom rendezvous later, she voiced her uncertainties. "It's all very worrying we don't know when it's likely to happen – I hope Jenny is going to be all right. How did you get on with Alastair?"

Bringing her up to date, Arthur thought back over their conversation and what had been decided. At her nudging, he woke up with a start. "I'm sorry, if only we knew what they're up to, we'd have something to go on."

❧

He was not the only one to voice that heartfelt wish. Waiting for their boss that night after the bank had closed, Turk was in a similar state of uncertainty. Sharing his concern with his cracksman friend, Jimmy, he complained, "He'd better come up with a plan soon. This time-wasting is driving me nuts. What with that berk Conway cosying up with that fancy Nancy of his, whispering away like a couple of lovebirds, it's enough to give you the creeps."

"It's all right for you," Jimmy said heavily. "Seeing all those green bucks slipping through me mitts every day is giving me the jimjams. Oh, thank gawd, here he is, at last. Well, what's news, boss?"

MacDougal wasted no time in getting down to business. "That scheme of mine bumping up the deposit interest has paid off, you'll be pleased to hear. They've been queuing up all week, falling over themselves to hand us their takings. They couldn't get any more in that strong-room if they tried."

"Lovely grub," chortled Jimmy, hitching his chair closer in his eagerness, "when do we start?"

"I was going to wait until that Jenny bird came and the coast was clear, but," he strummed his fingers on the table, "I've decided we can't afford to wait any longer. For one thing, we've lost our biggest customer – the ones who supplied our new electronic equipment, so we'd better clean up before anyone else decides to do the same. Not that it should worry us, there's enough loot in that strong room to keep us in luxury for the rest of our days. But more importantly, that creep Conway has put paid to that now with all his snooping. I'll deal with him later."

His tone left them in no doubt what he intended to do about it.

"Let me bounce him one," begged Jimmy.

"No, we haven't got time for that. Listen, this is what I want you to do." He drew out a plan of the office. "As soon as we close the doors at 12:30 on Saturday, I want you, Jimmy, to empty the tills at the counter – give them some excuse about doing a spot check, anything that sounds feasible, then get the money into the strong room. At this point, Turk, you get the rest of the stiffs to my office, say it's for a meeting, then lock them up and help Jimmy and myself to get the loot out onto the trolleys. Okay?" They nodded intently. "Good. As soon as we've got most of the stuff out, I want you to nip around to the back and keep the engine running on the hearse while we load up."

"On a hearse?" Jimmy looked fogged. "Gee whiz, how do we stash the boodle away in that kind of wagon, boss? I don't get it. You can't hide that much in one of those things without anyone getting their peepers on it."

MacDougal snorted at his inability to grasp the obvious. "Why, in the coffin, of course, dumbo, where else?"

"That's great," allowed Jimmy, grappling slowly with the idea. After a few minutes, he passed a hand over his fevered brow. "But what do we do about the geezers in the office?"

Their boss frowned. "If there's any funny business, we'll have to tie them up – but with a bit of luck, we'll be miles away by then. Any more questions?"

After taking it all in, Turk argued, "How are we going to get all that money in the coffin? Will there be enough room?"

"Good question," MacDougal answered promptly. "If not, I've got another hearse on standby around the back, but I hope we won't need it."

"But who's going to be driver if we have two of them and look after the loot as well?" persisted Turk.

"We'll worry about that when we come to it," was the confident reply. "Now you just remember what you have to do. I'll see to the rest. Don't worry about a thing – nothing's going to stop us now."

But despite his assurances, events were to prove him wrong.

Just as the cashiers were tidying up their tills, the front doors were pushed open despite Stuart's efforts to close them, and the agitated body of George, the butcher's assistant, threw himself at the counter demanding attention.

"Hey up, shop!" he called out. "Where is everyone? I want to see the manager."

Leaning across the counter, Alastair demanded irritably, "Oh, it's you, George. Not now, you ass. What do you want, I'm cashing up."

"Here, that's no way to talk to your customers," complained George. "Where's the manager."

"What do you want," repeated Alastair impatiently, "we're just closing."

"He promised me he'd get me on the local Chamber of Trade and I still haven't heard anything – not a sausage."

Turk appeared at his elbow and hissed. "Tell him it's being seen to, only get him out of here – get rid of him."

"That's not good enough," objected George stoutly, over-hearing. "I want to hear it from the manager himself."

Drawn by the arguments, MacDougal appeared looking harassed. "What the devil's going on here?"

Turk whispered in his ear, and the manager straightened up. "You can rest assured, sir, that we are doing all we can," he promised smoothly. "It will be dealt with as a priority, take my word for it."

"That's all very well," carried on George, oblivious to the mounting tension, "that's what you said the last time I asked."

"I tell you, I've written to the Chamber of Trade, and they'd promised to look into it, I can't do more. Now, do you mind, we're in the middle of an important meeting."

"It's not good enough." George was getting quite heated by now. "I gave you a choice cut off the joint last time you promised. I won't be satisfied until you've showed me the letter. Where is it?"

"You'll have to take my word for it," snapped MacDougal, beginning to lose his temper. "I must ask you to leave. Stuart, show this gentleman out."

Resisting strongly, it took the united efforts of Stuart, the messenger and the chief cashier to usher George out, still protesting as he went and calling out to his friends for help at the top of his voice.

Looking at his watch, MacDougal swore to himself. "Damnation, that's all we need." Turning to the cashiers, he snapped, "We're losing valuable time – carry on with it and get your tills agreed. This is upsetting all our plans... I mean, it's putting staff time at risk," he corrected himself hastily. "If we get any more of this, I can't answer for the consequences. Just make sure that door is shut before anyone else sneaks in."

But the words had hardly left his lips when there was a furious banging on the door, and instinctively Stuart opened it to see who it was and in came Jenny.

Rushing up to the counter, she waved to the manager. "Sorry to be so late, I got held up in meetings, do forgive me. Now, where do I start?" Her eyes picked out Doris as if to say, 'you still here?' and rested on Nancy with relief. "Stay there; I'll be right over."

To say that her arrival was greeted with enthusiasm by the manager was short of the mark by two or three continents. At the sight of Jenny, he started to panic, imagining for a moment that he was once again in the desert surrounded by a horde of enemy closing in on him from all sides, and moreover, he was beginning to feel events slipping out of his control. Moistening his lips, he forced a smile. "Good morning, Miss Young, you could have chosen a more convenient moment as we are extremely busy, but as you see our new equipment is working perfectly well, so there is no need to take up your valuable time."

"I'm so glad." Jenny brightened. "In that case, you won't mind me checking just to make sure. Hello, Nancy, you quite happy about everything?"

Nancy shot a helpless look of appeal at Arthur, but he seemed dumbstruck, terrified of making the wrong move and desperately anxious that his love would be able to get away while there was still time, in case the crooks changed their plans about the robbery. Eventually, he stuttered a reply. "Fine, just fine."

Jenny flashed a polite smile in his direction. "Good, then which one will we look at first?"

Getting a nod from MacDougal, Turk got up quickly. "Try mine, miss," and hurriedly took up a position next to his boss, ready to quell any rebellion that might arise. As if to reinforce matters, MacDougal tapped his watch meaningfully and muttered, "Don't let her go..."

Intercepting the signal, Arthur was put on immediate alert, fearful of her safety, and waited with bated breath.

"It's working beautifully." Jenny smiled sweetly and stood up, at last, looking uncertainly from Doris to Arthur. "Who's next?"

"Miss Leeds?" MacDougal motioned in her direction, trying to speed things up. At his signal, Alastair hurried over to stand in front of Doris protectively and received a tremulous smile in return.

"Lastly, Conway, if you please." Jenny waited uncertainly.

As soon as she sat down, she caught sight of a note left there hurriedly by Arthur who stood back hastily, looking straight in front of him, afraid he might give the game away.

Hiding a quick gasp, Nancy quickly edged in front to prevent anyone noticing. Taking in the message, Jenny's hand shook as she read the warning, 'Get out – it's a bank raid.'

Turning pale, she got up slowly and let go of the message as if mesmerised. In vain, Nancy made a grab at it, but it eluded her and fluttered to the ground. Instantly, Turk swooped and picked it up and without saying anything passed it to the manager.

"So," breathed MacDougal heavily, "it appears that I was right, after all, Conway."

Pretending not to hear, Jenny looked around the tense faces and tried to pass it off as if nothing untoward had occurred. "Well, that winds it up – thank you so much for your cooperation everyone. I think I'll be getting along now and allow you all to get back to work."

"I'm afraid we will have to postpone your departure for a while, Miss Young," decided MacDougal abruptly, nodding at his henchmen who moved up, blocking her exit.

"But I have another appointment – in fifteen minutes." Jenny glanced at her watch and faced him bravely. "I mustn't be late. What will they think of me?"

Taking advantage of the situation, Jimmy eagerly cast aside his role as first cashier and grabbed hold of her. "You're not going anywhere, baby."

Fighting him off, Jenny slapped his face. "What are you doing? Don't you dare touch me, you beast? Help, Arthur," she appealed.

Jimmy leered at her. "Don't bank on it, sweetheart."

Unable to stand it any longer, Arthur lunged at the crook and, grappling with his opponent, pinned his arms behind him in a half nelson.

"Jeez, get him off," howled Jimmy.

At a nod from MacDougal, Turk stepped forward and swiped at him with his blackjack. Taken by surprise, Arthur staggered and, releasing his victim turned around, ready to defend himself when he noticed the gun pointing straight at his midriff.

Hearing Doris scream in the background and feeling he ought to be doing something about it, Alastair squared his shoulders gamely. "By George, I'll show you, you scoundrels." He was about to join in the battle when he caught sight of the weapon and prudently changed his mind. Seeing Doris in distress, he rushed over and held her in his arms, doing his best to comfort her and shooting a glance at Turk as if publicly asserting his rights.

"Oh," Jenny cried out, forgetting all their past differences in a flash in her eagerness to let Arthur know how she felt. At the same time, in spite of her aversion to her half-sister, she couldn't help feeling secretly pleased that Doris had, at last, found someone else to claim her attention. She tried to reach out to Arthur to let him know about her change of heart but was forced back and made to join the other members of staff being rounded up in the background, including Harris who had just woken up.

Reluctantly raising his arms, Arthur stood there half-dazed and allowed himself to be frisked and moved back with the others. "You'll never get away with this," he said flatly, measuring his distance, debating whether to make a dash for it. Before he had a chance to do so, the manager anticipated such a move and waved at his accomplice irritably. "Take this lot away and tie them up in my office where they can't do any harm while we get on with it – we've lost too much time as it is."

As he watched them file past, he added viciously, "I don't care how tight you make it, especially with that menace, Conway. The tighter, the better as far as he's concerned. If it wasn't for him, we'd be miles away by now. If you want me, I'll be in the strong room." Feeling happier for getting that off his chest, he strode off.

12

NO ROOM IN THE HEARSE

As the door closed behind them, Arthur squirmed and wriggled on the floor where he lay, trying to free himself from his bonds. In the end, he rolled over in desperation and started rubbing his face up and down against the desk in an attempt to dislodge the gag knotted tightly around the back of his head. Finally freeing himself with a gasp of relief, he spat out the remains and immediately tried to do the same to the person next to him, who turned out to be Nancy.

Coughing and spluttering, he tried to heave himself up but fell back exhausted and groaned. "What an idiot I was. If only I'd got in touch with the police straight away instead of talking it over with Alastair. Now there's nothing to stop them getting away with it – if only I'd listened to you."

"Wait, there's still a chance." Nancy did her best to console him. After a fit of coughing, she hesitated then admitted, "I thought you might decide to do that, so I left a message for that detective you told me about, telling him to contact you."

"You what!" he said weakly. A surge of hope engulfed him. "What did you say?"

"Only that there was some trouble in the bank and could he

get in touch with you at your digs. I didn't say anything about Alastair," she said defensively. "I hope I did right."

He had a sudden vision of how Ben would greet the detective and found himself laughing for a moment at the thought. "No," he assured her gratefully. "I'm glad someone here had the sense to do the right thing. Now," he made a more determined effort, "I must try to see to the others. I only wish I could be there to see it happen," he added blissfully. "He doesn't know what he's let himself in for."

Unprepared for the day's dramatic events ahead, Detective Sergeant Bird checked in at the desk when he arrived at the office to see if there were any messages for him. Sifting through automatically, the one that caught his eye had the name 'Conway' pencilled on it.

"Hmm," he pondered, "that sounds familiar. How long has this been here, Sarg?"

"Let me see, must have been before I came on – sometime last night, I believe."

"Conway," Bird repeated, "that rings a bell. Wasn't he the one involved in that funny bank robbery recently?"

"Now you come to mention it, I believe you're right, sir. I think I've still got the report filed away somewhere – ah, this is it." He passed a copy over. "Something to do with a runaway truck. According to the manager, nothing was stolen, luckily. Here we are, two witnesses who were present seemed to have foiled the attempt – Alastair Stringer and Arthur Conway. You were right, sir."

"Thought I was." He fingered his chin. "Might look in and see what it's all about. Have we got an address for him?"

"Yes, sir, he's staying at digs with... a Mrs Musgrove." He leaned over confidentially. "A right old bossy boots, I gather."

"Where's that, Eustace Street? That's interesting, not far from here, I see. Such a glorious day, I think I'll take a walk – good exercise, they say."

"It's what I need, sir, stuck at the desk all day."

Bird took another look at the note and reflected. "Hmm, 'trouble at the bank' did he say? Well, I'll be off. Let the others know where I am."

"Yessir. Hope it's not another false alarm – we seem to have our full share lately."

"You can never be sure where banks are concerned," Bird commented. "Hmm, Mrs Musgrove. Let's hope she knows something about it."

If he thought Mrs Musgrove might be a good starting point, he was in for a disappointment when he got there. All she seemed to be worried about were some mysterious padded movements going on overhead. Applying her habitual 'fingers to the lips' policy, she opened the door cautiously, evidently hoping it would be someone else. "Oh, I thought it was our lodger, Mr Conway." She appeared flustered.

"Is he not in?" enquired Detective Sergeant Bird.

"No, sir. May I ask who is enquiring?"

The Detective Sergeant introduced himself. "I have a message to contact him. Can I come in for a moment?"

She opened allowed him in reluctantly. "I have to be careful because of him." She nodded upstairs fearfully.

Scenting a mystery, he lowered his voice. "Are we alone – is it safe to talk?"

"As long as you don't raise your voice," she said with a quiver, jerking her head towards the staircase.

"Is Mr Conway expected back soon?"

The landlady said brokenly, "He should have been back hours ago – we are that worried."

"We?" enquired the detective alertly.

"Me and all the lodgers," she whispered. "We don't know what to do."

"Are you in any danger?"

"Oh, that we are – all because of him."

Thinking there may be an intruder lurking in the background, Bird looked around quickly.

"Where is he?"

"Up in his room – don't disturb him, whatever you do."

"Is he dangerous – shall I fetch the police?"

"No, for heaven's sake. Mr Conway knows how to deal with him." She stood there, twitching.

"Is Mr Conway's room upstairs?"

She nodded fearfully.

"Can I go in and wait for him?"

Mrs Musgrove trembled. "On no account, I beseech you. I daren't go anywhere near it, in case he hears."

Bird raised his voice formally. "In that case, I must insist."

"No, no, I beg you. Colonel, Percy!" she called over her shoulder. "Come quickly."

A soldiery figure appeared behind her and close behind came Percy, peering over his shoulder. "Anything wrong, m'dear?"

"This gentleman wants to go into Mr Conway's room," she explained nervously. "He's a police officer."

A note of alarm sounded in the Colonel's voice. "Go into his room – is he mad?"

"Don't let him near that...mmm...menace," stuttered Percy, all of a twitter.

"I can assure you, sir, there's nothing to worry about – it's purely routine."

"Routine?" muttered the Colonel. "Does he know who's up there?"

Mrs Musgrove trembled. "No, I didn't like to mention – in case he heard."

The Colonel took over. "See here, Inspector…"

"Detective Sergeant, sir."

"Well, whatever it is," he said, irritated. "On no account can we allow anyone to go in that room until Mr Conway returns. You don't understand what he might do – he could be dangerous."

"Ab… absolutely," added Percy nervously, shutting his eyes at the ghastly consequences.

"He?" asked the Detective Sergeant quickly. "Do you need reinforcements?"

The Colonel snorted. "More like a tank squadron. You wouldn't catch me going anywhere near Ben unless he's on a lead and I'm in an armoured suit, and that's flat."

"You mean, he's a dog?" beamed the detective. "Well if that's all you're worried about, I'll deal with him. Lead me to him – I'm used to dogs. Why, I've got one of my own." He laughed, amused at the very idea.

The Colonel, Percy and Mrs Musgrove exchanged horrified glances.

"I'm sorry, officer," she said quite firmly. "I – we cannot allow you to do any such thing… until Mr Conway gets back."

"On no ac…count." Percy backed her up feverishly, barely able to get the words out.

"But I must insist," said the Detective Sergeant, pushing past.

"Colonel, do something."

"You don't realise what might happen if we let that monster loose," panicked the Colonel, aghast at what might happen. He racked his brains for an excuse, then harking back to his own encounters with the police in his youth, he stood there puffing and suddenly a distant memory came to his aid. "Have you a warrant, officer?"

"Well, no," admitted the officer, "but I wouldn't have

thought this might be necessary. This is getting ridiculous. Surely you aren't afraid of a dog?"

Mrs Musgrove came over faint and the Colonel bristled. "Eh, what? Definitely. Look here, Inspector, I've served out in India, and I tell you I'd rather face a horde of mad dervishes than have to deal with that beast."

"Me t...too," added Percy, as if there had been any doubt.

Stepping back, the Detective Sergeant nodded. "In that case, I must ask you to remain here while I get a warrant to search the premises. Good day to you."

Keeping his promise, he was back in under half an hour, waving a warrant card in their faces.

Watching fearfully as the detective made his way upstairs, the Colonel, who was always fond of boasting that he never blinked in the face of danger, hurriedly pulled Mrs Musgrove and Percy into the television room and started piling up furniture against the door in a mad haste.

A few minutes later there was an uproar overhead, and a large shape hurtled down the stairs and out of the front door, leaving a dishevelled Detective Sergeant hanging weakly onto the banisters, with his tie and collar askew, shouting, "Stop that dog!" before collapsing.

On the other side of the door, the Colonel and Mrs Musgrove, together with Percy who was covering his ears, looked at each other with mixed emotions, before the Colonel wiped his face in relief. "Thank heavens, he's gone."

Waking up to her own personal loss, Mrs Musgrove chimed in, "What am I going to say to that poor girl about her darling dog," and more to the point as far as she was concerned, she wailed, "and what about my lovely nest egg?"

Hearing groans from the other side of the door, she pulled herself up bravely. "We must get help for the poor gentleman. Will you ring for an ambulance, Colonel. I dread to see what Ben has done to him."

~

Undeterred by any monetary considerations, Ben only wanted to be reunited with his mistress and, of course, a large bowl of biscuits. Quickly picking up the scent, he lumbered off in pursuit, weaving in and out of traffic, leaving scenes of chaos behind him. Pausing only to give a quick lick to the officer who he last saw when he was perched on top of a taxi, he continued on his way, leaving cars to toot furiously at each other in his wake.

Arriving at the bank, Ben hurled himself at the front doors in his eagerness to get in. The noise could be heard even in the strong room where MacDougal and his gang were busily stacking up notes of every denomination, packing them in boxes for easy handling.

As one accord, they paused to listen. "What the hell is that racket? Go and see," ordered MacDougal, pausing to wipe his face. "We'll have the rossers around our necks if they hear that noise."

"Okay, boss, I'll deal with it," announced Jimmy hastily. "You carry on."

He threw another bundle in the box and squeezed with difficulty past the laden box to get to a window in the office and peered out. "Jeez, it's that damned dog again!" he called back. "What shall we do? Shall I plug it?"

"No, Turk, go and help him. That's all we need. Lock the brute up somewhere, where he can't get in the way."

"Okay, boss," obeyed Turk sighing, wondering how he had come to get mixed up with such a crazy set-up. He hastened to the door, joining Jimmy, and they wrestled with the bolts.

Before they could slide them back properly, there was a furious battering and Ben burst through, scattering them to one side in his desire to get to his mistress.

Pulling themselves up groggily, they looked around help-lessly. "Which way did he go?" blurted Jimmy.

"I bet I know," answered Turk grimly. "Let's go and see." He led the way to the office in a hurry, leaving Jimmy to shut the doors. Directly he reached the manager's office he heard an excited babble of voices inside and drew out his gun as a precau-tion. The next minute he was shouldered aside and Jimmy wrenched the door open and rushed in. Seeing Ben frantically licking Jenny all over, the crook's eyes gleamed malevolently.

"I'll soon settle his hash," he threatened and whipped out his gun.

Taking a breather after his efforts, Arthur staggered to his feet and dived to intercept, grabbing at the gun to deflect his aim. In the struggle that followed, there was a sharp report, and Arthur staggered and fell back, sinking to the floor.

In the furore that followed, Jenny screamed and hurtled herself at Arthur, cradling him in her arms, murmuring "dar-ling" and smothering him with kisses.

Kicking Jimmy's gun away, Turk covered them all with his weapon at the ready. "Jimmy, pick that up – and you lot, stay where you are if you want to stay in one piece." He backed to the door, keeping a safe distance. "Jimmy, here's some rope I found outside, tie that brute up, and we'll lock him away while we finish off downstairs."

The job of tying Ben up took longer than they had antici-pated. After they left, someone whispered, "Don't look now, but they were in such a hurry, they forgot to tie us up."

Recovering slowly, Arthur attempted to sit up but was gently restrained by Jenny. "Just take it easy, darling. You had a nasty knock. Don't try to move."

Rubbing his head, he looked up bewildered. "Did I imagine it? I could have sworn you called me 'darling.'"

Kissing the top of his head, she murmured, "There's

nothing wrong with your hearing, you wonderful man. You saved Ben's life."

"Now let's get this straight. D'you mean I get called 'darling' every time I stop someone having a go at Ben?"

"Darling, he did more than 'have a go' at my lovely Ben. That horrible man might have killed him. I could kiss you for that. In fact, I think I will." So saying, she held his face and gave him a prolonged kiss. "Don't you think he deserved it?" she asked the others. "I won't let him go now, whatever anyone might do to stop it." She glared defiantly at Doris as a challenge. There was a chorus of applause, and she turned beaming to Arthur. "Does that answer your question?"

For an answer, he held her face in his hands and asked nervously. "Does that mean you'll marry me?"

"I thought you'd never get round to it. Of course I will."

There was another round of applause, then Doris sat up and gave her approval. "That's okay by me, Sis. Sounds like they're not the only ones to do the right thing, eh, darling?" She glanced up at Alastair coyly.

"Eh, what?" the object of her affections looked alarmed, seeing his reputation as a confirmed bachelor going up in smoke. He loosened his collar nervously. "I say, it's a bit sudden, what?" He was saved from answering by Nancy, who had been absorbing the conversation.

"I don't like to spoil the party," she pointed out, "but does anyone know how Ben got here?"

"By heavens, that's a very good question," Alastair said, grasping at the straw being offered like a drowned man. "You were supposed to be looking after him, weren't you, old lad?"

"I left him with the landlady." Arthur frowned. "She promised to see to him until I got back." He turned to Nancy hopefully. "That note you left for the police – d'you think they may have let him out?" Not waiting for an answer, he clambered to his feet a little unsteadily. "Anyway, we can't hang around here waiting for them to turn up. We must do something."

"Such as what?" MacDougal appeared at the doorway with a gun, waving it at them menacingly. "Who left you lot untied? Turk, Jimmy!" he bawled down the corridor, his nerves fraying at the way events were sliding out of control. "Where the hell are you?"

A flustered Turk lurched in, out of breath, his hair ruffled. "Sorry, boss. It's that damned animal – we had a fight on our hands. Jimmy's dealing with him."

Jenny was on her feet, distraught. "I hope you haven't hurt him."

Turk snorted. "Hurt him – why that brute nearly killed us."

"Well, never mind about that," snapped MacDougal impatiently, "is he locked up out of harm's way? Good. That's all I want to know. We've wasted too much time as it is. He'll have to stay here – there's no room in the hearse. Get this lot tied up and make sure they don't get free this time and help me get the rest of the stuff loaded. Is the wagon still round the back?"

Turk nodded. "All ready and waiting, boss."

"Right, get to it."

"I'll leave you to do that little exercise," said Turk glancing meaningfully at the rest of the staff herded together in the small office. "Make a good job of it this time."

"Don't worry," growled Jimmy, fingering the thin cord he was handling lovingly. "They won't be able to move an inch after I've finished with them. Who's first, youse guys?"

Stuart held out his wrists. "If I may most bold as to offer, sir."

"Don't come the old butler stuff wiv me, son, or you'll get what's coming to you. Hold de mitts out and no back lip."

Watching Jimmy clumsily wrapping the cord around his

wrists, Stuart observed civilly, "If I might suggest, the normal procedure is left over right."

"Don't give me that." He wrenched at the cord savagely. "Keep your trap shut, or I'll plaster you all over de floor."

"Most distressing for you, sir," agreed Stuart, composing himself as best he could wedged against the radiator.

"Dat takes care of you, sunshine." Jimmy gave a final pull on the cord and leaned over menacingly. "One more wisecrack out of you, and it's curtains, get me?"

"Quite so, sir."

Temporarily disconcerted by the unaccustomed mode of address, Jimmy woke up to the fact that Arthur was about to grab at his ankle and jumped back, whipping his gun out.

"Can it, buster. That does it – you," pointing the gun at Stringer, "get off your ass and tie this lot up, while I keep an eye on you. Jump to it."

"I say, what, me?" Alastair climbed to his feet outraged and took the cord thrust at him.

"Hurry up, slowcoach," Jimmy threatened, looking at his watch and scowling. "This ain't a picnic party."

"No, I'm dashed if I will." Alastair drew himself up with some of his old spirit.

"This says you will – and put a shift on, buster," he said, jabbing his gun at Alastair's chest. "I'll give you ten seconds to make up your mind. One, two..."

"Do as he says," implored Doris, holding out her hands, "or he'll kill you. He means it."

"...three, four, five, six, seven, eight, nine..." He held the gun against Alastair's head, waiting expectantly.

"Please, darling."

"Oh, all right." He took the rope and apologised. "Sorry about this, old thing."

"Tighter," yelled Jimmy as Alastair proceeded to wind the cord around Doris's hands.

"We haven't got all day!"

Some fifteen minutes later, Jimmy waited, fretting, for Alastair to painstakingly finish his laborious task. "Now you, buster, turn round and hold your hands out. Hurry up, blast you." He pointed his gun as a shout floated up from below.

"Here, I say," complained Alastair, "not me as well, dash it... can't we come to some civilised arrangement?"

"No time for that, buster," replied Jimmy, casting a quick glance around. Without pausing, he whipped out a cosh and zapped Alastair, hurriedly catching him and laying him out next in line to the others, to the background of shrieks from Doris. He quickly lashed his victim's unresisting hands together and, with a final wrench, stood back satisfied.

He was about to kick his captive for good measure when Turk dashed in, hauling a trolley behind him. "Got this up in the lift," he explained. "Quick, load them up, we haven't got time to drag them downstairs."

"What all seven of 'em? How are we going to manage that?"

"Don't argue – give me a hand. We'll do it in two trips if necessary. Before you do that, make sure you gag them, mutt, otherwise they'll be yelling their heads off once we get going." Jimmy moodily complied, complaining, "Why don't I give them a tap on the nut – that should keep them quiet."

"Fat lot of good that would do – here, you take one end." Together they started lifting the bound figures one by one, but in the end, they stood back defeated. "This damn truck isn't big enough – it's no good, we'll have to do with just three of them and come back for the others," Turk decided, wiping his face.

Directly they arrived downstairs and started lifting the first one into the back of the hearse MacDougal appeared, dancing with rage. "Don't put them in there yet, you morons. We haven't loaded the money yet." He gestured towards the loading bay. "Stick them in there and come and help me bag up."

Beginning to crack under the stress, Jimmy yelped, "Give us a break, boss, this ain't a perishing removals job."

"If you don't put a move on, dumbo, you're the one who'll end up being removed – breaking up stones in Dartmoor. When you've done that, bring the trolley up to the vault."

Silenced, the two of them hurriedly brought the rest of the prisoners down on the lift and plonked them down without ceremony, leaving them trussed up in a huddled group.

Inside the vault, as each bag was stuffed full, the pile grew higher and higher until even Turk called a halt to question their efforts. "Boss, how do we get all this lot stashed away? We'll never find room for it all."

MacDougal mopped his forehead and gave in. "Okay, perhaps we'd better get this lot in first and see how we go. Don't forget we have a second hearse on stand-by. Careful..." He gritted his teeth. "You moron, you've split one of the bags."

"Not my fault, boss," apologised Jimmy, "it fell off."

"Well, don't stop to pick it all up now," he ordered, as the notes started spilling all over the floor. "For Pete's sake, leave it and get the others loaded."

One by one, the bags were wedged in the coffin until it couldn't take any more and they had a job keeping the lid down.

"Get the other hearse up, Jimmy, otherwise we'll be stuck here all night," MacDougal decided reluctantly.

"Yes, boss."

"While he's doing that, Turk, give me a hand propping these bodies up inside to make it look as if they're family."

A few minutes later, Jimmy dashed up waving his arms, agitated. "Boss, we've got a flat – what are we going to do?"

It was the last straw. MacDougal was stunned at the news and exploded, "I don't believe it!" Then pulling himself together, he decided abruptly, "I can't wait any longer; otherwise, I'll miss the rendezvous. Here's the map reference for the landing strip. Turk, you'd better stay and repair that flat – you used to be a car mechanic – and while he's doing that, Jimmy, you'd better get the rest of the money bags loaded and make sure we don't leave anyone behind to give the game away." As he jumped into the driving seat, he added, "Don't forget to keep to the side roads, you'll be sitting targets otherwise. Perhaps it's just as well," he consoled himself as he let out the clutch. "We're less likely to be noticed going separately."

"Wait a second," bawled Jimmy, "you can't leave us in the lurch like this – it's not flaming fair. You're leaving us to do all the dirty work!"

"Don't waste your time arguing," warned Turk grabbing hold of his arm. "We've got work to do unless you want to end up in jug."

Frothing at the mouth, Jimmy called out all the names he could think of before turning back morosely and throwing his trusty artillery away in a temper at the thought of starting the weary job of loading the rest of their ill-gotten gains. Unfortunately for him, the gun went off as it hit the ground and he screamed as the bullet found its target and left him hopping on one foot.

His yells of agony brought Turk running to see what happened. "You stupid idiot, what have you done?" After examining the injury, he looked relieved. "You'll live, it's only a graze. Come on, I've fixed the tyre, let's get this lot aboard."

"Only a graze?" howled Jimmy. "Is that what you call it? How can I do anything with only one foot?"

"Well, it's either that or wait for the rossers," was the unsympathetic reply. "Come on, I'll give you a hand. We've got to finish packing. We're running out of time."

Hobbling and cursing, Jimmy helped to finish the loading, pausing only to give a groan of suffering as each bag was emptied and some of it landed on his foot.

Without giving a thought to the occupants propped up

inside, they climbed into the hearse wearily and examined the map.

"That's it." Turk sat back in the driving seat and switched off the panel light. "Norfolk, here we come."

No sooner had the dust settled in their wake than a police car screeched to a halt in front of the bank and the driver helped an unsteady Detective Sergeant Bird alight. Hammering on the front door, his two accompanying detective constables finally forced their way in. Making his way unsteadily through the open doorway, Bird hobbled in to witness a scene of devastation. Picking his way through a pile of scattered notes and empty bags, he came across blood bespattered signs of a struggle and a piteous whine issuing from behind one of the inner doors.

Before Bird could give a warning, one of the constables unlocked the door and out charged Ben, knocking them flying before recognising his saviour and bearing down on him and licking him all over. As soon as he got his breath back, Detective Sergeant Bird clambered to his feet weakly and ordered them to search the premises.

Not content to wait, Ben rushed around sniffing like mad in search of his mistress, pushing everything to one side if it got in his way in his search for clues. A shout from one of the constables at the back of the premises alerted his attention, and off he bounded, answering the call.

Joining his men in the back yard, Bird took one look at the trail of banknotes embedded in the tyre tracks and immediately alerted his staff to put out an emergency call summoning help. He was so engrossed in getting this done, it wasn't until one of the constables drew his attention to the fact that he realised Ben was no longer with them.

Jerked back to reality, he demanded impatiently, "Which way did he go?" Realising from their gestures what had happened, he swore to himself and rushing around to the front again was met by the police driver pointing excitedly up the street. "He's just passed me, sir, going like the clappers."

Leaving one of the constables standing guard, he clambered back into the car awkwardly, and in the excitement of the chase forgot all about how he should behave, and instead of following the calm dictates of official procedure as he normally would, he flung out his arm, yelling wildly, "Follow that blasted dog!"

13

THAT BLASTED DOG AGAIN

Nosing clear of London, Turk began to relax a little at the wheel.

"Keep your eye on the road," he instructed. "We don't want to take the wrong turning. Have you got that map reference handy?"

Nursing his injured foot, Jimmy complained bitterly. "Too right, I'm not likely to forget that in a hurry – it's the only thing that keeps me going."

"We'll make it, don't worry. I didn't go to all this trouble for nothing. Once we get to that airstrip, we've got it made."

"That's if he still remembers us, the big palooka. What's the betting he'll take off without us?"

"No chance. He wouldn't dare." Turk laughed derisively, putting his nagging doubts behind him. "Talk sense, he'll need us to help shift all that loot he's collected. He can't do it all by himself, stands to reason, he's relying on us to help him – even if he was in the SAS."

"So he says," snorted Jimmy. "You can take that with a can of sauce – anyway, it's all right for you, you didn't get your perishing foot half shot off."

"Stop complaining, mate, just thank your lucky stars we haven't got the rossers breathing down our necks. As long as we keep going as we are, we're sitting pretty. They'll never think of looking for a hearse in a month of Sundays, let's face it."

"And whose fault is that? If that ruddy boss of ours had given us a hand instead of scarpering off like that we'd be at that airstrip he was talking about by now – and he's nicked all the talent himself, the crafty devil," he said taking a look over his shoulder. "All he's left us with are those damn snoopers and that high and mighty butler who's so full of himself." His mind dwelt wistfully for a moment on the girls. "That one called 'Jenny' I rather fancied, I don't mind telling you – proper corker she was and plenty of go in her."

"Yes, she soon taught you some manners, didn't she?" laughed Turk scornfully. "That reminds me," he jerked his head sideways, "how are the others at the back? Make sure they don't get up to any funny business."

"Na," Jimmy twisted around complacently, "they won't be able to move a muscle after the trouble I went to with those knots."

"I hope so," said Turk, slowing up. "Look out; there's a road-block ahead. You've got them covered up?"

"You're darn right, I have."

Reassured, he pulled up and poked his head out of the window. "What's up, officer?"

A policeman on duty stepped forward and seeing the coffin inside touched his hat respectfully. "Begging your pardon, sir, we've been asked to keep a sharp lookout – something to do with a robbery in the City. Sorry to trouble you."

"Not at all, officer. I am sure you're only doing your duty. If I may carry on... we're a little late as it is."

"Of course, sir." The constable stepped back and waved them on apologetically.

As soon as they were clear, Jimmy let out a gusty sigh of

relief. "Jeepers, that was a close one. They've got a dragnet out already."

"Well, that tells us something," observed Turk thankfully. "They haven't cottoned on to the hearse yet, by the sound of it. Good thing they can't make a squeak back there."

Little did he know that Arthur was quietly wrestling with his bonds again. Only a moment earlier he had redoubled his efforts, hoping to attract the attention of the policeman at the roadblock. Now that they were on the move again, he took a deep breath and tried rubbing his face against the support stand in an attempt to dislodge the bandage pulled tightly around his head, then rested before resuming his efforts. He could hear from a number of restless movements nearby that Stuart had similar ideas. He didn't hold out much hope for Alastair on the other side who he imagined was still suffering after being coshed, poor devil.

He stopped to rest for a moment and listened to the conversation in front, hoping to learn more.

"Where are we now?" asked Turk, checking the petrol gauge. "We should be okay as long as we keep the speed down. Otherwise, we'll have the rossers down on us."

Jimmy studied the map. "Says here we've passed Waltham Cross, next stop – Ware."

"Where?" asked Turk distractedly, noticing a spot in the rear mirror getting larger every minute as they were speaking.

"Ware," repeated Jimmy crossly, spelling it out. "Are you deaf or something?"

"No, I was just trying to see... oh, no, I don't believe it!"

"Wot's up?" Jimmy swivelled his head around at the note of alarm and jumped at the sight behind them.

"It can't be." His voice shook. "I don't believe it. It's that blasted dog again."

"I thought you had him locked up?"

"Stop the hearse; I'll settle to him for good, this time." He pulled out his gun in readiness.

"Put it away," ordered Turk fearfully. "There's another road-block coming up. Don't let them see your gat."

Just as Jimmy put it away reluctantly, there was a shuddering crash overhead. They glanced at each other in a panic.

"He's up there – what d'we do?"

The hearse began to swerve wildly from side to side, leaving the two occupants terrified.

"Mind out! The perishing coffin's moving – we'll lose the loot," howled Jimmy as Turk fought desperately with the controls. "Can't you see where you're going?"

"His face keeps on peering at me," Turk cried defensively as Ben was dislodged for a moment from his perch and half slid down the screen in front of him, blocking his view.

"Get him off!"

Jimmy dug out his weapon again with a purpose. "I'll soon settle his hash."

"You damn fool, there's another roadblock – put it away!" His hand trembling, Turk rolled down the window in trepidation, hardly daring to look.

A sergeant who had been standing in front of a hastily erected barrier stood gaping at the spectacle as if he couldn't believe his eyes. Pulling himself together, he stepped forward and got out his notebook. "Excuse me, sir, are you aware that you have a dog sitting on your roof?"

At a loss for words, Turk spluttered and finally got his voice back. "Oh that," he laughed unconvincingly. "Yes, we had noticed, officer."

"Don't you find it a little unusual, sir?"

Turk moistened his lips. "If I might explain..."

"I'm sure we would all like to hear – go on, sir."

"The fact of the matter is," a note of inspiration came to him, "it was the owner's last wish..."

"Oh yes?"

"Her last dying wish... was to have her beloved dog accompany her on her final... journey." His words were accompanied by a sob as he pulled out a scruffy handkerchief,

at the same time taking a furtive peep to see how he was doing, whilst dabbing at his eyes.

Unimpressed, the sergeant consulted the message he had just received and asked casually, beginning to relish the situation. "The animal's name wouldn't be Ben, by any chance, sir?"

Jimmy started convulsively at the mention, and Turk froze, letting the handkerchief slip through his fingers, while at the back Arthur made a fresh effort to attract attention.

Turk swallowed. "Don't mind him, officer, he's just lost an old and valued friend – he's still very upset about it all. We all have our cross to bear."

"Don't we all," agreed the sergeant solemnly. "Hello, we seem to have acquired an audience," he added, shifting his gaze to the back of the hearse.

"It's her pet rabbit," Turk gabbled desperately, not daring to look, "she had a thing about pets."

"Quite a menagerie," observed the sergeant cordially, signalling to his companion. "Now, I wonder if you'd kindly step out of the car for a moment. We wouldn't wish your pets to suffer in any way, would we?"

Anticipating such a request, Jimmy heaved himself up abruptly. "Not me brother, count me out." He grabbed at the door handle and lurched out.

Seeing his move, Ben jumped down joyfully, intent on joining in the fun, landing on the back of the emerging fugitive and squashing him flat. By the time Jimmy managed to scramble up and try to make a break for it, he found he had left it too late. Hampered by his injured foot, he started hopping away, but before he could get very far, he found the constable had slipped the handcuffs on his wrists from behind, and to add insult to injury Ben proceeded to pin him against the hearse with a meaningful look in his eye.

"Isn't it heart-warming to see such devotion," remarked the sergeant, patting Ben's head encouragingly. "Now I wonder what other goodies we'll come across?"

"All right, officer." Turk gave himself up with a resigned shrug, seeing his plans in ruins and realising further resistance was useless. "You'll find the others are safe and sound inside."

"Let me see," said the sergeant checking his notes, "would you be Arthur Conway?" as the first of the captives climbed out, throwing away the remaining bits of rope and bandages and stretching himself stiffly to get his circulation back. "Perhaps you would bring me up to date with what has occurred?"

In a few terse words, Arthur did so. Looking at his watch, he asked anxiously, "Have you caught the manager yet, he should be there by now." He caught hold of the sergeant's arm urgently. "There's no time to lose! He's got Jenny with him – she's in terrible danger. The man's a fanatic. He's got the other hearse stuffed with half the bank's takings."

"Take it easy, sir, he can't get far. We've sent out a nation-wide alert, and all the normal exits are blocked off."

"You don't understand," Arthur urged. "He's making for an old wartime landing strip on the coast. He'll slip through your fingers if we don't hurry – every minute counts."

The sergeant checked the map reference handed to him and rubbed his chin. "Hm, I see what you mean – this sounds like an air-sea rescue job. Get in the car, sir – my constable will see to the rest. I'll tell you what we have in mind on the way."

"Have we got room for Ben?" asked Arthur anxiously. "He'll go mad if we leave him behind." As the sergeant wavered, Arthur added, "He's good at catching the villains."

"So I see. Okay, bring him along. I don't know how you're

going to fit him in, though. It'll be a bit of a squash; you'll have to hitch up a little."

"I'll do my best," began Arthur, moving over obligingly, and the next minute the dog sprang in, licking him all over. "Steady on, Ben," he cried, fighting him off. "Save that for Jenny." Hearing her name, Ben subsided happily on Arthur's lap, spreading himself over most of the back seat.

The car was about to move off when there was a furious hammering on the window and Alastair's face appeared. "What about me?" he cried. "Damn it, he's got Doris as well."

"Okay, hop in, we can't waste any more time."

"I should think so too, old lad. What I always say is…"

"What about Harris and Stuart?" Arthur cut him short, peering through Ben's thick fur.

"We can't wait for them," dismissed Alastair. "Old Harris was fast asleep when I left, and Stuart is probably trying to wake him up. I say," he remarked, squeezing in next to Arthur and sitting back comfortably. "This is a bit more comfortable than getting stuck in a hearse, what?"

"Mmmm," was all Arthur could manage, trapped by the thick fur in his face.

"That's better," said the sergeant, checking his report. "We've got a helicopter standing by at Cambridge where your friend Detective Sergeant Bird is waiting – just what we need."

"Just what we need?" echoed Alastair dismally. "I say, do we need to drag him into it?"

Recognising the name, Ben gave a woof of approval and turned to lick his face, an impulsive act that gave Arthur some temporary relief and kept Alastair quiet for the rest of the journey.

As their car turned in at the airport, a familiar figure stepped forward, checking his watch. "Ah, there you are. No time to lose, follow me in my car. We've got a helicopter waiting, plenty of room for us all." He stopped short, catching sight of Ben. "Well, mostly all," he temporised nervously leaning on his crutch for support, keeping a safe distance after his recent encounter.

The helicopter pilot was equally dubious, sizing up Ben. However, after a brief chat with Arthur and Detective Sergeant Bird, he accepted that fact that he had no choice in the matter and hurriedly allocated the seats.

"Make sure you spread the weight," he advised after they climbed in, casting a dubious glance at Ben as the aircraft starting rocking in response to the unexpected load. "All aboard? Fasten your seat belts, please. Have we got a fix on the landing strip? Good. Right, as soon as we get clearance, we'll be off."

After an exchange over the intercom with the control tower, he sat back waiting for the signal.

"I say," whispered Alastair, clutching his seat belt as the rotor blades began turning. "He's a bit young, isn't he?"

"As long as he gets us there, who cares?" snapped Arthur, worried at the time slipping by. Sensing his concern, Ben jumped up and gave him a reassuring lick.

The pilot said nothing but grinned. Pulling the stick back and under his sure touch, the helicopter surged forward and lifted clear. As the ground raced past them, the landing slip fell away, and the landscape stretched before them. Not the flat expanse they had been led to expect, but undulating areas of green fields, and as they soared up higher and higher, in the far distance a glimpse of the sea.

Eventually, nearing the area under investigation, the pilot pointed. "Is that the spot?"

Escaping Ben's embrace, Arthur stepped over legs and leaned across to get a better view. "That's it!" he whooped in the pilot's ear. "And there's the hearse drawn up alongside." His eyes scanned the scene, desperate for signs of life. Suddenly he espied the familiar figure of McDougal looking up, shielding his eyes against the sun. "That's the villain," he said, pointing accusingly.

Almost immediately, the manager turned and ducked out of sight as he clambered into the cockpit of the aircraft below.

"Don't let him get away," implored Arthur. "Be careful," he entreated, fearful in case Jenny and the others were already on board.

"Leave it to me, hang on." The pilot gestured and pushed the stick forward. They were all flung sideways as the helicopter tilted and swooped down, bringing the aircraft below to halt as they banked past. Once clear, they saw the aircraft move forward again, swinging around, preparing to take off.

Repeating the exercise, they saw the small aircraft waver then stop, and a figure dropped out of the cockpit and raced across the ground, disappearing out of sight into a thick clump of trees nearby.

Detective Sergeant Bird waved his stick in the air. "Got him," he grunted satisfied. "He won't get far now; there's a squad car on its way."

"Never mind him," fretted Arthur, "what about Jenny? And Nancy, of course," he added, craning his neck.

"And Doris, by George," chipped in Alastair, crowding behind.

"Sit down, or you'll rock the boat," instructed the pilot. "We're going in now."

As the helicopter manoeuvred into position, Arthur had to hang on to Ben, afraid he might upset the balance. Directly the rotors slowly came to a halt. Ben was straining at the lead again, sniffing at the door as if waiting for someone to open it. Knocking the pilot aside in his eagerness to get out, he surged forward, dragging Arthur with him until he ended up hanging onto one of the struts for support. Getting his breath back, he whispered in Ben's ear. "Go, seek Jenny," and released him.

Like a shot, the dog was off making a beeline for the hearse, sniffing and pawing at the doors in anticipation.

Getting up groggily, Arthur saw a line of policemen with tracker dogs fanning out, searching the nearby undergrowth.

Not bothering to stop, Arthur's only concern was to find Jenny and make sure she was safe. Joining Ben at the hearse, he wrenched a door open and choked back his relief at the sight of the three girls lying tied up inside, unharmed. Heaving Ben to one side, he gently lifted the nearest one out, helped by Alastair and the sergeant, with a group of policemen standing by, ready to assist.

As he cut her free and undid the bandage around her face, Jenny gasped with relief and flung arms around him. "Oh, Arthur darling, I thought you'd never come."

"Thank God you're safe." He buried his head in her hair, thankful he'd reached her in time.

"Hold it, right there!"

Bemused, he swung around, fearing a sudden attack, and the flashbulbs started exploding all around him.

"What, what?" he uttered bewildered. "Who are you?"

"Don't move! Hold that – it's great."

"Who the... what is all this?"

"This," said the grinning reporter, "is the story of the century. Don't you know? I'm telling you, your first words are going to be front-page news on the all the dailies, believe me. How do you feel about that?"

"Wait a minute." Jenny sat up. Taking in the situation a glance and struck by a brilliant thought, she tugged at Arthur's sleeve to claim his attention. Giving him a gentle nudge, she coughed discreetly. "Before you say any more, darling, you should remind these gentlemen that I am your, ahem, press agent, and that whatever you say will be an exclusive interview."

"Oh, rather," enthused Arthur, catching on.

Seeing his dream interview slipping out of his grasp, the young reporter said hurriedly, "I'll have a word with my editor, don't go away," and rushed off to report.

In no time at all, or so it seemed, Arthur sat back dazzled at the latest events. "He's arranged a press conference tomorrow in London for ten o'clock – I don't believe it!"

"Don't I get a thank you?" asked Jenny demurely, tracing a line on his mouth.

"Yes, yes, don't you realise what this means? Oh darling, I could kiss you."

"What's stopping you, darling?"

"Nothing," he agreed, folding her in his arms in a prolonged and satisfying embrace.

"I say, that sounds a good idea," Alastair joined in, unwilling to miss any opportunity. "Eh, what – a good bit of publicity?"

Doris, who up until then had received his undivided attention spoke up, aggrieved, "Hey, don't I have something to say about this?"

"Not now." Alastair quietened her with a gesture. "This needs thinking about. Arthur, my old mate," he said, massaging his friend's shoulder lovingly, "what say we go into this together? I can just see it now, written in huge letters, 'The Stringer-Conway Partnership,' we can't fail."

"I'm afraid, Alastair dear," Jenny interrupted sweetly, "that's already booked as a going concern. Haven't you heard – it's going to be the Arthur and Jenny partnership, isn't it darling?"

Their loving thoughts were interrupted by the Detective Sergeant hurrying up, looking frustrated. "Blast it, he's slipped the net."

"Oh, no," exclaimed Arthur, and Jenny shivered.

"Never mind." The detective relaxed. "We've recovered the

money he stole, and the other two have been rounded up with all their loot as well."

"So that's something else you can talk about tomorrow, darling," beamed Jenny, smiling fondly at her beloved. "Meanwhile, they're going to put us up in a hotel overnight – I can't wait for tomorrow."

14

A SPECIAL PRIZE

In the full glow of the spotlights and unused to all the sudden publicity, Arthur gulped and started off hesitantly, telling a hushed audience how he stumbled on the plot that led to the downfall of the mastermind behind the robbery at his bank and paid tribute to Nancy for her help in contacting the police.

At the conclusion of his speech, Jenny got up and announced, "I am very pleased to tell you that my fiancée, who is rather a shy person – and I love him for it, bless him – is an experienced freelance writer who will shortly be publishing an exclusive account of his investigations, something we will all be looking forward to, thank you. Now, the floor is open to any questions you may have."

At the end of the flood of questions that poured in, Jenny raised her hand and made an announcement that raised the roof. "Finally, I would like to announce a special prize that has been awarded by the insurance company that acts on behalf of my company, Automatic Machines Ltd., a major customer of the bank affected by the robbery. As a token of their gratitude for helping to track down the robbers, a special prize goes to my lovely dog, Ben, who has earned a mammoth basket of bones and a big cheque to go with it to keep him in food for many years to come. If someone would kindly lead him up to the platform, I will present him with a rosette."

Hearing his name announced and unwilling to wait for an escort, Ben shook off his handler and, scattering any photographers in his path, arrived panting at her side and looked up adoringly at his mistress.

As she sat relaxing with Arthur after the tumult of the conference died down and the press and audience had departed, a voice from the past broke into her reverie and made her gasp, and she nearly spilt her drink.

"Say, what a swell poodle you've got there, honey."

"What?" She wheeled unbelievingly. "It can't be – Daddy, is it really you?" Overcome by emotion, she jumped up delightedly. "Where have you sprung from? I can't believe it." She threw herself in his arms and eventually stood back to take a good look at him, getting over the shock.

He patted her on the cheek. "Yessir, it's your old dad, Harry S Young in person. I heard you were hot news on the wire and came right over. Who is this knight in shining armour I've been hearing about? No, not you, Ben, I know all about you," he said, backing off good-humouredly.

"Dad, may I present Arthur Conway – we're going to get married."

Harry seized Arthur and pumped his hand enthusiastically. "So you're the one they're all talking about. Congratulations. This calls for a celebration. Why don't we meet up at this hotel our Doris keeps telling me about, Whites, I think they call it?" Seeing her hesitate, he coaxed, "Come on, honey, this is my first chance to catch up on all the things that have been happening while I've been away. Say, I know, why don't we make a big event of it – hang the expense, it's all on me. Bring all your friends along and we'll make it a swell party. What about it?"

"Say yes," added a small voice next her. It was Doris. "Do say yes," she repeated wistfully. "It will give me a chance to say sorry about all those horrid things I made up about you and Arthur."

Pressing her hand, Jenny fought back a lump in her throat and made up her mind. "What a lovely idea, Daddy. We'll make it a family occasion, and I want all my friends to be there as well."

At the end of a sumptuous meal, their host stood up swaying slightly and rapped his spoon on the table to gain everyone's attention. "Looking around me," he beamed, "I can't tell you how happy this occasion makes me. Seeing my two lovely daughters together again fair breaks my heart. If only my dear wife, Gloria, was here to share it with me." He stopped, attempting to focus his eyes. "I feel so..."

"Happy?" prompted Jenny quickly.

"You've got it. No, not happy," he searched for a better description, and everyone waited anxiously with bated breath, "overjoyed, that's what I wanted to say," he triumphed. His words were greeted with heartfelt applause.

"And you know what?"

"Get on with it, Pa," urged Doris, seeing Alastair propping himself up across the table and helping himself to more wine – hoping she would be able to extract a proposal from him before he nodded off.

"I was about to say, before I was interrupted by my nearest and dearest, I have been so impressed," he swayed, raising his glass approvingly, "by these splendid surroundings that, gee whiz, I have decided to... you know what... I have decided to buy it... and hand it over to my daughter."

Doris jumped up excitedly, hand to mouth, and Jenny watched, mouth half-open.

"My daughter – Doris – to run."

There was a scream from Doris that half-woke Alastair and he glanced around sluggishly. "Whaa-at's up?"

Their host held up a hand solemnly. "Not forgetting my other lovely daughter – Jenny. Did you know," he peered around owlishly as if imparting a great secret, "she's marrying that splendid fellow, Arthur, um, something." He waved a vague hand. "Anyway, I'll see she has the same settlement the day she gets married." Having got that off his chest, he collapsed back on his chair, wearing a blissful smile of contentment.

Running around the table, Doris shook Alastair with glee. "Did you hear that, darling. That means we won't have to worry about money anymore."

At the mention of money, Alastair opened a bleary eye defensively. "Money? No, it wasn't me, it was head office who wanted it – eh, what?"

"You're not listening, darling. Daddy is buying this lovely hotel for me to run – for both of us. Now do you understand? You've only got to say the word..." She looked up at him beseechingly.

"Are we, I mean, are you, by George..." He made an effort to follow her. "Does this mean that you and I will be able to dine here for free – every day." His eyes lifted up to the ceiling as if witnessing the miracle of his gravy boat sailing into the harbour at long last. "In that case, my love," he slipped down awkwardly on one knee, "will you do me the honour..."

"Yes, yes, yes," she cried eagerly, not waiting for him to finish. "I do, I do, I do."

Rubbing his chin thoughtfully at the prospect, Alastair ruminated. "That means, if I get young George in as catering manager, I can get a fresh steak each day – and while we're at it, old Stuart would make a jolly fine head waiter, don't you think?"

"Anything you say, Alastair my love, anything you say." She nestled up cosily.

Witnessing the scene with relief, Jenny's hand stole out to Arthur's. "Thank goodness. That's laid the family feud to rest at last, my love."

Thinking over what Alastair had said, Arthur pursed his lips. "That reminds me, we've forgotten all about your friend Nancy – if it wasn't for her the police might never have known."

"Don't worry, darling, I've already seen to that. I've got my boss to give her my old job as supervisor; it's what she's always wanted."

"You think of everything, my love. I can't help wondering what might have happened if old Morrissey didn't get that promotion of his – he'd be perfectly happy doing his old job and playing with his trains."

Jenny sat up with animation. "Hadn't you heard? They've put him back in charge while they get the place back in a fit condition again. Just think, now you've been promised that whacking great advance you can sit back and get on with writing your great novel – you won't have to think about working in that place any longer."

"That's true," agreed Arthur happily and tried to imagine what it might feel like being landed back with his old job again in an empty office. "Old Morrissey will be a bit lonely though, with nobody to talk to all day."

The same thought had occurred to Mr Morrissey next day as he sat in his old office waiting for the work to begin. Struck by a sudden idea, he pulled out a drawer hopefully and found to his delight his half-forgotten station master's hat and whistle and his red flag...

Before you go...If you could spare the time, it would make all the difference if you could add a review, we'd love to hear from you. For more information, log on to the website where you will find details of the stories currently available as well as news of forthcoming publications.

ABOUT THE AUTHOR

Following National Service in the RAF Michael returned to banking until an opportunity arose to pursue a career in writing. After working as a press officer for several electrical engineering companies, he was asked to set up a central press office as a group press officer for an engineering company. From there he moved on to become publicity manager for a fixed-wing and helicopter charter company, where he was involved in making a film of the company's activities at home and overseas.

He became so interested in filming that he joined up with a partner to make industrial films for several years, before ending his career handling research publicity for a national gas transmission company.

Since retiring, he has fulfilled his dream of becoming a writer and has written two books for children as well as several romantic comedies.

You can read more about Michael on his website:
www.michaelwilton.co.uk and
https://www.nextchapter.pub/authors/michael-n-wilton

BOOKS BY MICHAEL N. WILTON

Introducing William Bridge

Losing his job at the local newspaper after depicting the sub-editor in a series of unflattering doodles, William Bridge is called on to help his uncle Albert keep his shop going. The first thing he does is fall in love with Sally, the latest shop volunteer, despite formidable opposition from her autocratic stepmother, Lady Courtney.

Following a break-in and lost orders, an SOS sent to Albert's maverick brother Neil for back-up support changes everything. On the run from the police, Neil disguises himself and encourages William to be nice to a visiting American security expert and his flighty daughter Veronica to promote business, causing a rift in the budding romance.

The pressure mounts for William to investigate rumours of a shady deal to take over the shop and threaten the life of the village. William is willing to pay almost any price in his desperate fight to win back his love and save the shop.

Amazon: <u>My Book</u>

Amazon UK: <u>My Book</u>

Goodreads: <u>https://www.goodreads.com/book/show/35402257-save-our-shop</u>

Once again, William Bridge must put aside his ambitions to become a writer and marry his sweetheart Sally when her father, Sir Henry, is involved in a scandal that threatens to put an end to the family's hopes of getting their son Lancelot married to the daughter of a wealthy American security expert.

Foiled in his attempts to get his own back, Foxey Fred and his gang find a new way of retrieving their fortunes by blackmailing Sir Henry who, fearful his wife may find out, appeals to William for help. Calling on his Uncle Neil for support, William sets out to unravel the threads of lies and deceit despite continued opposition from Sally's stepmother, Lady Courtney, and a series of female encounters that are enough to test the trust of even the most faithful admirers.

Amazon.com: My Book

Amazon UK: My Book

Goodreads: https://www.goodreads.com/book/show/40226784-in-the-soup

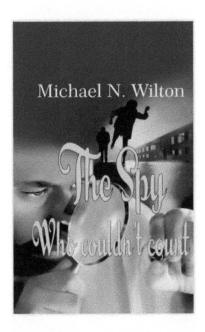

Inflicting Christian names like Jefferson Youll on a young lad already saddled with a surname like Patbottom is a sufficient handicap for anyone, but if you have the misfortune to be educated at somewhere like Watlington County Grammar and end up as thick as a plank and can't even count, life gets very tricky indeed. Settling for Jyp and braving a succession of dead-end jobs, he finds sanctuary in a Government statistics department dealing with figures, much to the hilarity of his father.

To escape the amorous attention of his ever-helpful colleague, Jyp panics and dives into another office where he is recruited by one of

Britain's security departments after a hilarious interview in which he is mistaken for a trained spy killer.

Despite his initial bumbling efforts, he takes on a fight to unmask a series of trusted spies in the heart of Whitehall in a desperate battle to win the hand of his true love.

Amazon.com: My Book

Amazon UK: My Book

Goodreads: https://www.goodreads.com/book/show/35997630-the-spy-who-couldn-t-count

When James Clipper, a retired merchant navy captain is nicknamed Granddad Bracey, after teaching his grandson Peter how to swing from the ceiling on his braces, he little realises that it will involve them in an epic adventure on a far-away planet called Seven Seas, where his granddaughter Sally, has to battle against all the odds to save her mother's life.

Amazon.com: My Book

Amazon.uk: <u>My Book</u>

Goodreads: <u>https://www.goodreads.com/book/show/25382531-granddad-bracey-and-the-flight-to-seven-seas</u>

When the animal wildlife in Hookwood is disturbed by the arrival of a young couple eager to set up their first home together in a derelict cottage, an inquisitive young rabbit called Startup decides to help out by finishing off their picnic lunch, donated by an old friend to celebrate the occasion. As a punishment, his mother Dora sends him out to look after his scatty friend, Clara Goose, while she moves house to escape the attention of the young couple's pet, a fearsome ginger cat.

After restoring the lifetime savings of his friends, dubiously acquired by Squirrel Nabbit, the rascally pawnbroker, Startup sets out to prevent Clara's nest egg falling into the hands of a smooth talking brown rat known as Captain Mayfair, who is looking for funds to back an uprising led by the fearsome King Freddie and his brown rat colony.

Amazon.com: My Book

Amazon.co.uk: My Book

Goodreads: https://www.goodreads.com/book/show/25385540-happenings-at-hookwood

You might also like:

Wherewolf by Tony Lewise

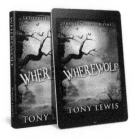

To read the first chapter for free go to:
https://www.nextchapter.pub/books/wherewolf

Don't Bank On It, Sweetheart
ISBN: 978-4-86747-479-2

Published by
Next Chapter
1-60-20 Minami-Otsuka
170-0005 Toshima-Ku, Tokyo
+818035793528

28th May 2021

Lightning Source UK Ltd.
Milton Keynes UK
UKHW011827170621
385713UK00001B/171

9 784867 474792